The Mask

of a

Marriage

The Mask of a Marriage

Prologue
A Damaging Encounter

Heath Gregory's gaze was transfixed on his wife's tensed face. Of course, there was the barrel of a gun in the way - rigid, black, and menacing - pointed at his chest. *Does she know it's me? How could she?*

He was heavily disguised, as was the rest of his crew, with elaborate masks that hid all facial features. Draped with a hood that tucked into his shirt, it prevented hair attributes from being revealed. The material was breathable and virtually transparent from one side, his mouth and eyes concealed without impairing their function. The mask itself was a carbon fiber work of art, molded to look like a Greek god (Zeus, had it been?), and painted gold. Two, durable elastic straps along the back secured it to his head and the base of his neck. Lastly, a voice modulator was implanted on the inside of the mask's mouth, lowering and mechanizing the tone of his speech.

"I said: put your fucking hands in the air!" Laura Gregory shouted across the four-foot gap between them. Morning sunlight flitted through shut blinds, bouncing off the clean faux-granite tile. Laura was an FBI agent, and a damn good one. Heath was always so proud of her determination and stubbornness to succeed at her career. She'd made a name for herself.

How and *why* she was here this morning though were questions that sent his mind spinning. The Seattle FBI office was close by, sure, but there was no reason for her to be in *this* bank *this* early. She'd been secretive of her recent projects because they were "Confidential" and "High Profile", but he hardly believed the FBI Special Unit was cracking medium-scale bank heists now…were they?

"Look man, drop the gun." Her voice had become calmer. An attempt to sooth her husband, the criminal. "You haven't done too much wrong so far. You can come out of this with your life still intact. I just need you to put your gun down and put your hands in the air. Slowly."

Heath caught sight of the sweat glistening on her brow. Beneath the mask - despite the tense situation - he smiled. He began to speak and the voice modulator took over.

"I'm not going to put my gun on the floor." The combination of the deep, mechanical voice and the mask with no moving lips terrified Laura, yet she remained stoic. "I will, *slowly*, slide my gun to my back and raise my hands."

"That's not good enough. Gun on the floor." She held firm.

"I'm not asking…" Heath replied, slowly shifting the weapon's strap along his shoulders. Laura's head cocked to the side briefly at that response. A minuscule motion. "So what happens now, miss…?"

"My name is Laura. What happens now is that you tell your boys to stop piling the cash away, we wait for my backup, while you remove the mask and lay on the ground. If all of that goes smoothly, you *might be* out of jail in less than five years time."

"And if it doesn't? Go smoothly, that is?" The question echoed like a haunt from the modulator.

"I will shoot you. And then it's anyone's game. But I promise you, I'm a good enough shot that you will not walk away from it." Laura paused. "I really don't want to kill anyone today, but I have before. Don't test it."

She's killed someone? Heath hadn't known this. He wondered when. *Way to be a present husband, Heath.*

"I don't want you to shoot me either, but we're not going to do any of what you're asking. I offer another route: you sit down with the other hostages - none of whom will come to any harm - let us go about our business, and we all move on with our lives. Alive and not in jail." Heath knew she wouldn't go for it, but it was now about buying time.

"You know I can't do that and my patience is wearing thin." She reaffirmed her stance and moved her fingers along the gun's grip. "Take the fucking mask off, now. I'm not asking…"

Ain't married life a bitch?

Part I
New Opportunities

Married life is a weird thing for a plethora of reasons. We're conditioned to believe that a lot changes once we tie the knot, but really nothing does. The person that you've (hopefully) known for several months or years is still the same. Your jobs are still the same. Your friends are the same. Your home. The things you enjoy doing together. The sex. Honestly, if anything is different at all, it's the unsettling notion that everything is likely to be the same for a very long time. Maybe forever.

Oh, and I forgot to mention the secrets we keep from each other. Those don't change either.

~~~

My secrets started before I ever met Laura. If anything, I feel guilty for bringing her into my world, but hey…that's love. How's the saying go? What she doesn't know won't kill her?

I never knew my mom nor did I ever find out what happened (if that's even the right word to use) to her. My dad was there, but not present. Not mean either, not demanding…just *there*. A living ghost. Growing up, I just thought he was quiet or sad, but nowadays we know very clearly that he was depressed. He had a deep-seeded mental illness that eventually won when he shot himself in his freshly-cleaned 4-door sedan, sitting in a half empty grocery store parking lot.
~~~

In an odd way, I missed him, but I didn't feel sad about the situation. I think I felt sadder *for* him. As his only son, and only remaining family, he left everything to me, but I was too young to take care of it on my own; only about 12. Child Services came for me often, but I was able to dodge them left and right. I'd already been basically living on my own for several years before my dad's suicide…why would I want to go to a group home?

It would be an understatement to tell you that the Child Services department in Des Moines, Iowa is not very good at their job. Evading them eventually became as easy as not answering the door when they knocked. Once I was 14, I was able to get a job - which I think they knew - so they didn't bug me much after that. I was still going to school too and I imagine my teachers were able to provide them periodic updates. If anything, it was my love for learning that probably kept them off my back.

I did well in school and it came naturally. I was behaved because…well…I just didn't see the point of being a jerk. My teachers liked me. I had "friends" inside the confines of the building, but rarely hung out or played with other kids outside of school after my dad died. In a way, my dad had subtly taught me how to *not* exist. Strange for kids my age, I got a lot of joy from learning and, for the most part, I had great teachers. I imagine most teachers are "great" when they have students that remind them why they got into teaching in the first place. I was that kid…I could see the long-term benefit of learning these topics and even the short-term rewards of favoritism from my teachers.

Anyway, I digress. My high school years were fine, unmemorable and uneventful, mixed evenly between working as a grocery store bagger, then a scanner. I was able to get a decent chunk of scholarship money to the good ol' University of Iowa and the Tippie College of Business. My goal was to focus on a collection of classes with an entrepreneurial lens, but my major was technically "Management". My college experience (which was far better and more "normal" than my childhood and high school experience) was cut short the day I met Bernard.

Halfway through my junior year, while most kids were back home and I was on campus for Holiday Break, he approached me. I was reading at a brewery in a booth toward the back. If I remember correctly, it was some sort of self-improvement book about time management and the beer was a seasonal pumpkin ale. This was a lazy afternoon without classes so I was enjoying my introverted time.

"What'cha reading?" Was the first time I heard that voice. Grizzled, but not in a "this guy's crazy" sort of way. There was an undercurrent of informal power. I looked up to see a man that appeared both old and young, his silvery hair and various wrinkles revealing the years, but the length and flow of said silver hair - along with a well-grown beard - was lush and vibrant. Rolled-up sleeves of a black Henley shirt showed thick veins along the forearms. Coupled with his general stance and demeanor, I could tell he was a physical specimen. *Was I being hit on by a dude?*

"Uh…" I'd forgotten the title so I turned the book over. "The 4 Hour Work Week."

"I can tell it's captivating." He pointed at it while he sat in the booth across from me.

"Ummm. Yeah." Why was he sitting down? "Can I help you with something?"

"I'm hoping you can, Heath Gregory."

The name drop was a clear power move. I shifted in my seat, slid my beer to the side, and placed the book on the table.

"Have we met?" I prodded, with some aggression woven into my tone.

"Nope. I just know who you are." He answered as if that wasn't the creepiest thing in the world. As if I was supposed to be comforted by it. I soon came to find out, that's Bernard for you! "Orphaned at 12 years old, generally just kind of a sad at-home life, but somehow you prevailed. Did well in school, stayed out of trouble. Managed your money, got some scholarships. Now you're crushing it in college too. Nobody to be proud of you except yourself, which is both depressing and awesome at the same time."

I wasn't a fan of the head games. Plus, I was three pumpkin ales in, "How the fuck do you know that? What do you want?"

"I want to offer you a job."

"Hello sir!" A waitress had eagerly approached Bernard. She studied him briefly, likely some college co-ed wondering if he was a sugar daddy. "Can I take your order?"

"What're you having?" He pointed to my beer with a lazy finger.

I responded tersely. "The pumpkin ale."

"Nice. I'll have one of those please."

"Great. Can I see an ID?"

"Oh! You flatter me." This strange man flirted while he pulled out his wallet. I tried to glance at the square piece of identification from across the table for any clues, but the whole process was too quick.

The girl giggled as she gave it back. "Thank you, sir. I'll have that right out."

The man I now know as Bernard turned back to me. "Where were we? Ah! Right, I want to offer you a job."

"Not interested." I started to chug my beer and made as if I was aiming to leave. This guy was creepy, probably wanting me to do some sort of sex thing. Or drug thing. Or a sex *and* drug thing.

"I think you're going to be. Please, just hear me out. If you're truly not interested at the end, you'll never need to hear from me again."

"Fine. Get me another beer and I'll give you 10 minutes."

The waitress came back beaming, placing his beer down on the table.

"Can we snag another for my friend here?"

"Sure thing!" She returned quickly and Bernard began explaining the proposition that would change my life.

"I rob banks." He paused briefly, waiting for my reaction. I didn't give him much more than a raised eyebrow. "I like to just come out and say it to get it out of the way, not to mention, I come off pretty mysterious with the whole 'I know who you are' bit."

He talked a lot with his hands.

"You're the kind of person we look for in this line of work."

"Why?" I hardly believed him.

"Because you're smart. Both books and street smart. Plus, you don't have very many people in your life. Sucks, but that makes it easier for you to not need a cover story all the time."

"Ok, but why would I do this? I don't know you, I've never stolen anything before, *and* it's highly illegal." I can't lie: I was mildly interested as I took a swig of the aromatic, amber beer, not knowing why my attitude had suddenly turned.

"Because I can make you stupidly rich." Bernard started. "What famous rich people don't tell you is that they'd rather be crazy rich, *anonymously*. Rich without all the attention, followers, etcetera. Most of them anyway…

"The way we do things, the anonymity is a *necessity*. There's no other way. My crew and I have gotten very good at doing this. I'd go so far as to say we're the best in the world."

I snorted, even if I partially believed him. He caught up to me and drank his beer.

"So, you're telling me an orphan from Iowa is the best you can do to join your crew?"

"Probably not, no. I'm sure we could find someone better. But we want you, friend."

"Why do I feel like that's missing 'to be our sacrificial lamb' at the end?"

"No one in my crew has ever gotten caught and I intend to always keep it that way."

For a moment, we sat in silence as I thought about the proposition more.

"How rich are we talking here?" It was the question burning brightest in my head.

"I'm worth about $300 million." Bernard offered. "Off the books, of course."

"Holy shit? What're you stealing? Nuclear weapons?"

"That's the beauty of it. We aim 'low'…medium sized banks with available cash. Then we have a *very good* advisor who puts our money to work. Most of that $300 million is from growth of what we stole."

"Ok, I'm in." I spat out. Either this guy was the best liar I'd ever seen or I was about to join a prosperous crew of bank robbers.

"Great. What're you doing this weekend?"

~~~

The next several months were a blur and it turns out Bernard was telling the 100% truth. He was adamant I finish college, both for my own wellbeing and also to avoid suspicion. But I quit my campus job within two weeks and was soon meeting with the team almost every weekend. They quickly became the family I'd never had, despite all the cliches that statement comes laced with.

There was Jazz, who was somewhere between Bernard and I's age, often outfitted in a dark hoodie and shorts that showed off his intricately tattooed legs. He was our "IT" guy, meaning he was responsible for all the technology which, to be completely honest, was often over my head and was an extensive responsibility. "Tech" didn't just cover *our* technology, but also scoping out the technology we'd be up against: the bank's security systems, the local police, and more. Despite being our nerd, Jazz was a cool dude and one of my favorite people to drink and talk about life with. I eventually came to learn he was an Australian citizen with some Samoan heritage mixed in.
~~~

Jasmine was our "Fashion" expert, but that would be diminishing her role, even if she liked the title. From Saudi Arabia originally, she was dark skinned and had an ever-changing hair style with her luscious, black locks. When I first met her, it was shoulder length, equal parts wavy and messy.

Every heist had strict restrictions for uniforms and coverage techniques, including masks themselves. Bernard was passionate that every small detail should be covered, meaning that Jasmine often had the unenviable task of figuring out ways to make us subtly alter our physical appearance (height and weight) while designing functional, unique, and intimidating masks. She was our group's free spirit; often providing the optimistic opinion to counteract any instances where group cynicism was prevalent in heist planning.

Then there was me, essentially dubbed Bernard's protégé. That could have pissed the other two off, but they always welcomed me with open arms without any semblance of jealousy. Bernard was basically the "Strategist" and had been finding that it was turning into a two-person job. "Strategist" was a fancy way of saying "Project Manager" and included things like scoping out potential targets (both online and in person), creating timelines for the heist, identifying key dates along the way - including the day of the heist itself, and the tactics that we'd use to pull the whole thing off. It was that last part that I found was especially difficult and rewarding, thanks to Bernard's rules:

8 Rules of the Heist:
1. Have a cover and keep the silence
2. Never use the same tactic within the same decade
3. 2+ years between heists. Allow cool down time
4. No ego amigo. Modest scores only
5. Never replicate masks
6. No killing
7. No one gets caught (though if someone does, they'll get 50% of everyone else's cut for that heist)

8.   Invest! The "big" money comes from what you do with it after

We memorized and lived by these rules. They were our code and they bonded us. Outside of the four of us, this whole thing was like *Fight Club*…we didn't talk about it. Not even to our close friends or partners, though I wasn't sure anyone in the group had much of a dating life aside from the occasional "fling". Before Laura, I didn't either. Our lack of connection to other people outside the circle kept us focused and motivated. I had joined the group at a pivotal time. They'd just completed a heist in Istanbul without any issues. They had laid low individually for nearly five months, and the time was upon them to begin planning for their next one, likely over 24 months away (per Rules of the Heist #3).

School and any accompanying social life faded to be a distant afterthought. I lived alone on campus and had zero friends. My college experience was laughable, but I was consumed with the intricacies of planning something as risky and complex as a bank heist. The challenge was immense, and because of it, school came easily - almost *too* easy - to where I could skip class all together and still pass. Bernard eventually noticed this and pulled me away from my strategic responsibilities for a time. I, of course, was furious, but he was right; I needed a better balance. To this day, that's been our only argument and I respect him for setting me straight.

~ ~ ~

Eventually, the target of their next heist (my first) narrowed in on Austin, Texas. Jazz and Jasmine (in case you're wondering…she hated going by "Jas" for short) were not stateside residents, so the scouting landed on Bernard and myself. Not only was it part of our specific responsibilities, but traveling from Iowa to Texas was a quick plane trip away. We were about 18 months out from the planned heist date - I had just wrapped up my junior year of college - when Bernard and I took a joint trip to San Antonio, Texas and traveled by car to Austin during the day. Even that small step made us harder to track should anyone ever be investigating, especially once the heist was complete, and it was these subtle details I began to learn and absorb from Bernard. Our cover was as a father and son, spending some quality time together. In many ways, it was exactly that. We enjoyed good food and drinks in the hot summer weather, and even took in some of the city's sights. Most of our scouting was planned in our hotel rooms using old fashioned pen and paper to jot down the banks and addresses we would check. Our day's plans would be a reflection of various banks along a specific path of which we'd saunter past, perhaps enjoying some ice cream or a coffee. We had a lot of coffee on scouting trips.

Test 1 was to scout for initial feasibility. A lot of things Google Earth and Maps could tell you: general traffic patterns, closest highway, nearby police stations, and the lay of the land…but it was often much different seeing it in person. Foot traffic was important as well as surrounding buildings and their viewpoints. Brief assessments of camera positioning was critical. If Test 1 checked out, the bank in question would move to **Test 2:** drone reconnaissance.

Bernard has a special photography license for drone flying (likely fake, I've never asked) and we would station ourselves at a nearby park, acting as tourists. Jazz had modified this drone to be wickedly quiet and have immense range. The camera was outfitted with 64x zoom with 8K resolution and a suite of filters (infrared, electromagnetic, etc.) to spot more intricate details about the bank's security systems. It was in **Test 2** where most banks would fail out of the process for some reason or another.

The final cleverly-named Test, **Test 3** was done in person and required precise caution. We were careful to only do one or two per city; anything else could be seen as suspicious. Our approach had to be the same in each: inquiring about opening a checking account, interest accrued in a money market, ATM location maps, etc. They must match so it would look like normal customers doing mundane research. We'd never go in pairs and each time we wore a hidden camera to record everything for later dissection. These were invaluable final pieces of on-site reconnaissance because they provided a view of the interior, an understanding of their personnel, a better grasp of the exits, windows, and logistics, and a feel for how busy they might be at any given time. As rules go, an informal one was that any in-person research meant the heist date was *at least* six months away.

On my second trip to Austin, I was tasked with doing in-person research for our likely target, while Bernard was completing another. Beforehand, he had coached me on what to look for, the do's and don'ts of "acting natural", and how long I needed to stay to allow Jazz to work a back door into their security system. My scouting was uneventful and further confirmed this bank was perfect for our future heist. It hit all the boxes: lower grade security system, "big" enough that the reward was worth it, minimal foot traffic in the morning, and a layout free of very many corners, allowing us to keep an eye on everyone.

Emerging from the bank into the sun-drenched and cloudless day, I realized I didn't need to meet Bernard for several more hours. The morning was mine to explore Austin or - even better - find a local coffee shop and read a good book. I turned the corner of the squarish, terra-cotta colored building.

And that's when I ran straight into her.

"Ha! Oh damn, I'm so sorry!" Our bodies had bumped chest first into one another, hers somewhat blocked by an arm holding a phone, studying a map.

"Oh my gosh! That's what I get for staring down at my phone." She didn't seem the least bit offended I had accidentally (I swear!) grazed her breasts in the collision. For the briefest of moments, she looked up to acknowledge me and continued to follow her path, determined.

I wasn't so quick to move on. Her summery perfume enraptured my nostrils and lingered. Crystal brown eyes matched smooth, almond skin. A flowy, short sun dress gave way to defined legs, arms, and shoulders; she was clearly into fitness. Luscious hair cascaded partway down her shoulders, free and semi-messy. *What was she so concentrated on?*

"Excuse me, miss?" I decided to shoot my shot.

"Hmm?" She turned and brought her face up from her phone, taking me in for the first time. I'm not sure what I was expecting, but I was disappointed as there seemed to be no semblance of mutual attraction running through her mind.

"Where are you headed? Do you need help?"

"Oh…I. No, I should be fine." Her phone dinged and distracted her for another moment. "Oh my God, seriously?"

"What?"

"Sorry. Without going into all the gory details, I'm here for a bachelorette party and the maid of honor is a total bitch." The gaze of those brown eyes re-met mine. "Sorry for cursing."

"Don't be. I can only imagine." I pointed over my shoulder. "I was going to find a local coffee shop, want to join me?" *Say yes…say yes…say yes…*

"You know what? Yes. Fuck Chrissie. She can rally the girls on her own. The bride won't even be here until tonight."

"Yeah! Fuck Chrissie!" It came out perhaps *too* enthusiastically. "Sorry."

"Don't be." She smiled and walked toward me. "She sucks."

The impromptu date obviously went well. Nearby was a quaint coffee house filled with small plants, sunlight, air conditioning, and one hell of a pour over. Laura got a cold brew with almond milk. Our banter was electric, almost as if we had known each other for a while. I made sure to listen and ask thoughtful questions. I was no expert at first dates - they made me incredibly nervous - but I knew enough to let her do the majority of the speaking. We ended up staying long enough to split a chocolate chip cookie…then get late morning cocktails. Eventually her phone was blowing up enough that she couldn't ignore it any longer and had to get going. Apparently, Chrissie was "freaking out". We trash talked her a few moments more before she asked for my number, which sent my stomach flipping. I gave it to her and she texted me right then and there.

Sadly, our first time together was short, but we both felt enough energy to keep texting and conversing over the next several weeks. It was hard balancing school, planning a heist, and courting Laura, and there was more than enough times Bernard made me turn my phone off, or some combination of Jazz and Jasmine would give me shit. As someone who's young and in love often does, I completely over-analyzed everything, my new career direction being one of them. Should I really be in this line of business if I wanted a girlfriend? A family? As I alluded…cart before the horse. At this point, my attention was a pendulum, swung fully in the direction of Laura.

That is, until we started talking numbers.

"The target for the Austin heist is $2.5 million, each." Bernard stood next to our massive whiteboard with a big red **$3M** circled on it. Jazz and Jasmine didn't seem phased, but I distinctly remember nearly crapping my pants. "I've got the Advisor on the line, and he'll explain what the more accurate number is."

By "Advisor", he really meant "Financial Advisor" and he was the person Bernard had to manage all of our money. We never knew his name, nor had we ever seen him, in-person or virtually. His voice was freakishly trustworthy and his knowledge deep, layered, and specific. This guy knew all the basics, where the world economy was going to go, where it was dead, and how to keep us anonymously rich. It was a condition of working for Bernard, that the Advisor had to manage your money, so we didn't really have a choice.

Drunkenly, I pressed Jazz and Jasmine on it one evening and they both had the same reaction.

"Trust the guy. He will make you richer than you can imagine, and it *never stops growing.*"

Back in our planning room, the Advisor began his high-level explanation.

"After the heist, we'll keep that money on ice for six months to verify it has no tracking mechanisms built in. As you all know, banks do this to varying degrees and we usually lose anywhere from 1-3% of the total haul because of it.

"Your money will be accessible to you after that point, but per usual, I recommend not touching it. I've got several investments lined up, including a new-ish entrant dubbed 'cryptocurrency'. Small stuff now, but it may have a flash-in-the-pan moment, we'll see. Besides that, I've done the usual rigor to determine stocks poised to breakout or stocks poised to crash that will eventually recover. Longer term, I'll commit a portion of each of your hauls to our real estate portfolio, which now sits at over $50 million in properties that my team manages. As always, if you have specific questions or want advice on expenditures before you make them, don't hesitate to reach out for some one-on-one time." His spiel ended once he added, "Especially you, new guy. Let's you and I talk so I can get a feel for your goals and spending habits."

As a pretty-much-broke college student who had lived most of my life bordering on poverty in Des Moines, Iowa, having a financial mentor, much less having millions of dollars for him to help me manage was unbelievable. In that moment, the pendulum of my attention came dramatically back to the heist at hand…and all future heists with this group.

It was lucky for me that Laura wasn't fazed much by my slower replies and diverted attention. I explained to her that work and school was crazy and she understood - and was equally passionate about her schooling. She explained she was in Denver going to school for Criminal Justice, with a minor in International Studies. According to her, it was a strong combination if she wanted to join the FBI, which was a driving passion of hers. I specifically remember thinking that was silly at the time. Joining the FBI always seemed like one of those childhood dreams akin to "I want to be an astronaut", but in reality, it was me subconsciously hoping it didn't work out for her. If I was going to rob banks for a living, I couldn't be with someone who was with the FBI, could I? That felt like oil and water, but it wasn't something I could exactly broach and I was far too cowardly to end things over it.

A month had passed in our relationship and we acknowledged it had stalled out. We'd been texting with a handful of video calls, but it was clear we needed to see each other in person. We were both on the cusp of wanting to define "us", and it felt weird to do if we'd only had a single coffee date under our belts. We both wanted to reinvigorate and judge the live chemistry. Our wanting needed validation. Iowa City, despite being a college town, isn't exactly a "destination" spot - plus Denver sounded way cooler - so I traveled to her.

Somehow, she was able to get her roommates to leave town that weekend so, suffice it to say, we had a lot of fun. The brief connection we'd experienced in Austin was increased tenfold and the physical attraction and sex (I assume you want all the tantalizing details) was the best I'd ever had, even if that was a very short list.

Not mentioning anything about robbing banks was the hardest part. This was where I began my new skill I'd eventually need to perfect: *lying*. What was I supposed to do? We were falling for each other. I officially asked her to be my girlfriend on that visit…it wasn't like I was about to implode everything because I had the opportunity of a lifetime that was "illegal".

Ok, fully illegal, no quotes, whatever.

We kept the trips frequent, almost monthly, which helped us grow closer, while allowing me to focus on the heist, with school on the side. Bernard, gruff and seemingly angry one day, approached me about Laura.

"You're playing with fire, Heath." He started as he began splitting pistachios from their shells, eating them. "She's studying to join the FBI…what exactly do you see happening here?"

"How did you know that?" I pressed.

"It doesn't matter. It's true, isn't it?"

"Yes."

Jazz walked by the two of us, noticing the intensity of the conversation, and scurried along faster.

"Does she know about us? About this?"

"Absolutely not. I know the rules."

He cracked a couple more shells with his rugged, thick hands and ate the nuts before starting again, apparently calmer. "Look kid, I like you. There's a reason you're here. Obviously, I'm not telling you to never have another romantic relationship. That's not how I want you living your life. But this one is particularly risky."

My only reply was a hung head, staring at a speck on the table in front of me.

"I want what's best for you, but I will also put you out, no questions asked. Don't put me in a position where I'll have to do that."

"Yep, got it." I stood to leave and Bernard didn't stop me.

I deserved the scolding and warning. If anything, it made me take the secret all the more serious. I spent time after that honing my excuses…my cover stories…my core narrative. If I wanted Laura and the heists to work, all of this had to be airtight. Perfect. Always.

The day of the Austin heist, my nerves were out of control. Jasmine had a remedy to that…literally. She concocted some syrupy, tasteless liquid that we each took a swig of; common practice for this crew. It was supposed to reduce your heart rate and support brain function. I felt like it did nothing, even with assurances it was working as intended.

Through our investigations, we'd discovered the bank's vault walls were not exactly up to code, likely because it was part of an older building. Somehow the bank branch hadn't needed to update them (or they'd paid a fine and moved on with their lives) so the heist didn't require anyone to actually enter the bank, per say. Instead, we set off the fire alarm to push the patrons and employees out, while simultaneously blocking the call to the fire department and police. This was where Jazz came in, accomplishing this remotely. The confusion created a 30-minute window for us to work with, drilling through the wall into the vault. It was noisy, but no one was around to hear because of the alarm.

Although we had no interactions with other people, we still wore masks, just in case. This was my first experience with Jasmine's elaborate and functional designs. Our wardrobe was all black, but we were each given specific body-morphing elements. I had shoes with padded heels that gave me an extra two inches, for example, while Bernard's clothing was baggier to create the appearance of being skinny. The masks themselves were black ballistic headwear with white-painted patterns on each. Stripes, shapes, swirls…the designs were elaborate and the masks fully covered our head and hair, never to be used again.

Luckily, that was all unnecessary as the heist was executed without a hitch. Jazz, monitoring the cameras of the connecting businesses and buildings said we never even appeared on a single frame of footage. It was truly a bank with a significant design flaw that we took advantage of and someone else probably got fired from.

I was grateful for my first time being smooth and conflict-free and once the $2.7 million hit my bank account - and I had a good, long talk with the Advisor - I was hooked.

I was now, officially, a bank robber.

Fucking crazy.

Laura and I's relationship continued to blossom in the weeks following the heist. We visited each other more often; she came to Iowa and fit right in at the local college hotspots. I quickly learned that she effortlessly commanded a room, whether she wanted to or not. People watched her, wanted to talk to her. Wanted to be her friend…or more. If I hadn't recognized it before, I was incredibly lucky.

Weeks turned into months.

Those months turned into years.

I graduated from the University of Iowa and its business school with a degree in Business Management. I wouldn't need it, but the accomplishment didn't feel as hollow as I expected. I was relieved I had a fallback option. I was proud I'd done it. Sure, I now had Bernard and the crew, and, more importantly, Laura…but before them I had done this "life" thing on my own.

Laura, being the superstar she is, graduated with honors from DU and had already started conversations with the FBI. After an extensive interview process, they brought her in at an entry level role with the promises she would quickly move up as she proved herself. Spoiler alert: Laura crushed it and was quickly promoted to owning her own task force…more on that later.

I, of course, continued with the heists. As I watched my first haul of money grow with excitement, I became more and more locked-in to this lifestyle. Our Advisor knew what he was doing. I could trust him. I could trust Bernard. Jasmine. Jazz. We were like a happy little family. A family that was planning a bank robbery in London, but a family all the same.

And I learned that I was *good* at this. Really good. I had Bernard's guidance of course, but otherwise I essentially planned the entirety of the very complicated London heist we dubbed "The Presidential Bandits". The name stemmed from the elaborate masks of U.S. Presidents we wore and I imagine historians find some sweet irony in the metaphor of American Presidents stealing from their allies across the pond. Unlike the smoothness of Austin, London's day-of-action had complications. The weather didn't cooperate. There was an unusual amount of people at the bank that day. Jazz ran into tech issues. The ever-reliable Tube, our escape route, was running behind schedule. But we all kept cool heads, problem solved in-the-moment, and made it out with no one in jail. Because there were witnesses, the heist was more high-profile than our previous one, but all of the chatter we gathered afterwards suggested the authorities were grasping at straws trying to identify culprits. Eventually, headlines shifted across several news cycles and the London heist was a faded memory for the public and a dead-end investigation for detectives.

For us, it was a windfall of cash. Bernard said it was their biggest haul yet, and for that very reason, the next heist would be smaller.

"This is about managing the heat on us, not beating our own records. Let the Advisor make you rich, not your ego." We all agreed, with fervor.

Our next heists were in Malta (smaller) and Sydney (somewhere between Austin and London size). I could write a whole book about either of those. Sydney in particular got quite hairy, but we came out the other side whole. That was three years ago now and I've been robbing banks with this crew for slightly more than a decade now. I'm worth nearly $100 million and our crew collectively is close to a billion. With a 'B'!

Throughout all of this, Laura and I remained together, eventually getting married. Bernard was less than enthralled, but had since given up the argument. It created a silent tension between us where, should it come to it, he would drop me without hesitation if Laura's connection to the FBI endangered the team. Jazz and Jasmine were more outwardly happy for me, but I knew it made the entire group uncomfortable. Luckily, I was indispensable by this point and it was buried deep within the group's collective psyche.

To protect them, I'd perfected my lie to Laura over the years. According to her, I was a well-paid analyst on the international expansion team of a healthcare corporation. It's a remote role with 30% travel, allowing me plenty of excuses for any heists and their planning. Over the years I've made myself very familiar with the healthcare industry of the U.S. and countries we expand into, aiming to wear her down with the minutia of my day-to-day. I know what I'm talking about when I lie, and she tapered off long ago asking about my job. It bores her.

If I'm being honest, I think I disappoint my wife with my disguised lack of ambition for my job. She's continuously pushing herself at the FBI while I've remained an analyst for years, not wanting to move up because then it forces me to craft a different set of lies. It may pique her interest again. We're in a safe spot right now, but it saddens me to think she perceives me this way…especially when there's over $100 million (and growing) waiting for us to find the right time to disappear.

~~~

There's a deep part of me that hopes Laura and I can make it as husband and wife until I ultimately reveal the truth to her. Beyond wondering how she'll react, I have concerns about our marriage. Ones that I keep bottled up. My crew (read: friends) don't want to hear about it because it's a point of contention in the first place, and I feel held back from broaching it with Laura. Outside of that, I don't have anyone else to talk to.

And I'm continuously second guessing if this is just…normal? Our relationship isn't bad, it's just boring. We don't fight or argue, but we also rarely have sex. Our conversations feel surface level and mostly circulate around Laura's job. Lately, she's been working on more classified
~~~

material so even that topic has been removed from the table. We don't really go on dates anymore; maybe to a brewery once in a while. But more often than not, she's drained from work or we just end up sitting on the couch watching pointless TV while looking at our phones.

I can't remember the last time we've taken a trip together.

We have no pets.

There are no kids in the picture.

It feels like we're biding time until *something* happens. For me, that something is telling Laura everything. I wonder often what that something is for her.

The dreary and sullen Seattle weather doesn't help either. We live here now because it's her station: the Seattle FBI headquarters in the city. But there's another added benefit to living here at the moment…

Downtown Seattle is the location of our next heist.

Part II
More Than a Job

I love my husband, Heath, but something feels like it has changed in our relationship…in our marriage. He feels intensely focused, almost all the time, but I couldn't really tell you what he's focused on. It's not me, it's not our friends, and it certainly doesn't seem like his career. He's been in the same Senior Analyst role for years and while they pay him good money with plenty of cushy work-from-home perks, I barely know what he does. At any other company, it would be time to leave - to look elsewhere - but I generally keep my mouth shut. Perhaps it's some hobby I don't know about that's diverting his attention.

That's the thing about marriage: the unknown, the *secrets*…they fester.

The thing about me is, I don't have any fucking time to worry about those secrets.

At least not right now.

~~~

Being a black woman, I could sit here and tell you about a hard upbringing I had to endure to get where I am today, but that's just not my story. I was lucky to be part of an affluent family that lived in a suburb of Denver, Colorado. Sure, I was the only little black girl in a 10-mile radius (probably), but my parents were loving people with good, boring jobs, and I attended a decent school, making quality friends along the way.

My best friend was (and is) my brother, Jason. We're only separated by a couple years - I'm the oldest - and we never
~~~

really had the sibling rivalry thing. Weird, I know, but chalk it up to our parents raising us well. Particularly in grade school, we would play together all the time in our yard and around the neighborhood, until the sun started to set. It was a different time back then, but nightfall was still our "curfew" if we weren't already at home doing homework.

I remember that our favorite game to play was "Spies". I don't know if I was enamored by just how boring and indescribable my parent's jobs were, or if it was all the old James Bond movies we'd watch with our dad, but "Spies" was what my brother and I would play all the damn time. We'd hold our own fists with a pointer finger out, or use some misshapen twig as our "guns" and basically just create the narratives as we went along. We were brother and sister spy, working for a top-secret organization to take down the bad guys! The bad guys were whoever was on the news at the time because we honestly didn't know anything about the world. Russians. Terrorists. Drug runners or gangsters. They were all groups we had to infiltrate.

We'd spend hours making up fake investigations, hiding in cover, rolling around in the grass to the next piece of cover, and - near the end of every session - was an all-out imaginary brawl. Kicks and punches and wrestling with some invisible enemy. Our favorite thing to do was yell "Back-to-back!" where we'd lean our backs against one another out in the open, green lawn, and turn slowly, waiting for ghost punches and kicks to send us into a tizzy.

I can't say our parents were thrilled with the violent undertones of killing a bunch of imaginary bad guys, but it kept us busy and out of their hair, plus there were worse things we could have been doing. Eventually, Jason and I grew out of it (me before him), but something about the sentiment stuck, deeply rooted in my thoughts and purpose.

The thrill of the hunt.

Of the secrets.

I didn't know *exactly* what I wanted to be when I grew up, but I at least knew I wanted it to be related to investigating things.

As I grew, being a super-secret agent for the CIA (or God-knows-who?) seemed unrealistic and less sexy, but something like an undercover detective with a police force, a CIA analyst, or an FBI task force agent all felt within my grasp. I'm a driven person and this goal became very real to me the second I started high school. Not many students can say that, but I had done enough 8th-grade-level research to get the message: I had to do well in school for a lot of "next steps" to unlock.

In high school my main focuses could be summarized as: school and soccer. I was naturally gifted at that specific sport (clumsy as hell in others) and it was my outlet. All the pressure I'd put on myself could be let out at practice, or during games, and it helped keep me sane when school would kick my ass. It didn't come easy to me, but I also recognize I had a great support system. Loving parents, supportive teachers and coaches, proper materials and books to learn, etcetera.

Going to college was bittersweet for a host of reasons, but I knew it was the next critical step in the career I wanted. I gave up soccer to focus on school (and, let's be real, I wasn't talented enough to make the team) and moving away from my family - mainly my brother - was a bummer. Luckily, the University of Denver was only 30-ish minutes away so I was able to visit often. And eventually, I grew into my own at DU, had a close-knit group of friends, while my brother had gone away to school in California (typical Jason).

Many would scoff at my college experience, but I wouldn't trade it for the world. DU is a smaller school, but they still can party. I did have my fun, but made sure I earned it too. Work hard, play hard mentality I suppose. School was my sole focus, followed closely by working out. With soccer out of the picture, I was passionate about staying healthy and got into weightlifting, something that helped to clear my mind and center me. My circle of friends was next on the priority list while partying, drinking, and boys were all in a distant third place, though they had their moments.

I majored in Criminal Justice with a minor in International Studies; a pretty lethal combination when trying to get into the line of work I was scoping out. The classes were consistently intriguing, and much like my schooling thus far, I really enjoyed *learning*. Naturally, my competitive side emerged, and becoming top of my class was a target I had in my sights.

That is, until I met him…

~~~

Oh my God, Chrissie! I swear, I'm going to punch her in that mousy mouth of hers if she doesn't calm the fuck down. I literally just stepped off the plane and already have three texts.

- Where are you?
- Have you gotten into downtown Austin yet?
- We have an emergency!

Once I was off the plane, I politely texted back, "What's the emergency?"

"Steph's flight has gotten delayed!"

Ok, that could be bad. "By how much?" I sat there, annoyed, as the gray bubbles of her reply bounced around in their oval.

"An hour! At least!"

Chrissie was an idiot, plain and simple. As the maid of honor, she had been acting like more of a bridezilla for this bachelorette party than the bride. I'm sure it wasn't me, but I wondered how Steph was even friends with this girl.

"Chrissie, that's not that bad at all. Happens all the time." I sent. "I'm heading into the city now. I'll let you know once I'm near the hotel." *Maybe.*

I continued to watch as her gray bubbles bounced around again. They stopped. No reply.
~~~

God she's dramatic.

Traffic was light and I'd only needed a carry-on so getting into downtown was a painless experience. Even my cab had been a silent affair, just how I like it. The hotel was near the Texas state capital, one of my favorites. I was a bit of a geography and state capital nerd in elementary school so seeing the distinctly pink granite glisten in the daylight took me back. Something must have clicked right then because I remember thinking, *Fuck Chrissie. I'm going to drop my stuff off at the hotel first.*

As if she could read my mind, I got a new text, sent to the whole chain.

"SOS ladies! I'm headed to the place where we're having dinner tonight. I called to double check and they say there's no reservation. NOT OK. Let's all meet there in 30 mins to show them how important this is to us!"

I wanted to scream, but instead laughed as another bridesmaid, Kendall, privately messaged me a gif of a comedian putting a finger-gun to their head. We were all beholden to Chrissie because Lord knows she was going to rat us out to Steph should we not play our part. This led to me quickly unpacking what I could in my early-arrival room to head back out into the day.

Within moments of leaving the hotel, head buried in my phone, I passed the corner of a building, and ran straight into a man. My phone (and his arm) hit my tits, but I knew immediately it was my fault. He said something inaudible that I couldn't hear through my embarrassment.

"Oh my gosh! That's what I get for staring down at my phone." I was sidetracked and really thought nothing of the chance encounter, quickly looking up, not really seeing him, and continuing on toward the God-forsaken restaurant we were supposed to rally against. I'd only made it a handful of paces before he called to me.

"Excuse me, miss?" *Ugh.* What does this bozo want?

"Hmm?" I turned and finally looked at him for more than a nanosecond and I remember thinking: *Son-of-a-bitch!*

He's gorgeous. But keep your face straight, don't give it away. I always liked to play hard to get.

The young man before me had to be around my age, likely still in college. If he went to college? Was he from here? His face was boyish with the amount of stubble - just past five o'clock shadow - that I like. His short, brown-blond hair made him look even younger, but the deep brown eyes felt like they held wisdom from hardships. Something about their gaze…And whatever shirt he was wearing was doing it for him. Clearly fit, he was thin, not bulky, yet his muscles still revealed plenty of veins pressed under his tan, slightly sunburnt skin.

"Where are you headed? Do you need help?" He asked politely. *Laura, snap back to reality!*

"Oh…I. No, I should be fine."

My phone dinged again. All I saw was an ALL CAPS: "LAURA…" before I couldn't contain my eyeroll any longer.

"Oh my God, seriously?" I sighed.

"What?" The nice guy's fake curiosity asked.

"Sorry. Without going into all the gory details, I'm here for a bachelorette party and the maid of honor is a total bitch." I felt bad for the outburst as our gaze caught. "Sorry for cursing."

"Don't be. I can only imagine." There was an ever-so-brief awkward pause and he motioned behind him. I caught his bicep bulge beneath his shirt. "I was going to find a local coffee shop, want to join me?"

I shouldn't, but why the hell not. Am I really going to let Chrissie cock-block me? Steph isn't even here yet.

"You know what? Yes. Fuck Chrissie. She can rally the girls on her own; the bride won't even be here until tonight."

"Yeah! Fuck Chrissie!" I almost laughed out loud at his camaraderie. "Sorry."

"Don't be." I was genuinely impressed and started in the direction he'd pointed to. "She sucks."

Over the next several hours, we had one of the best and most casual first dates I've ever been on. The coffee house had been beyond cute, with plenty of greenery dressing the walls and shelves while my cold brew was one of the best I'd ever had. Sure, it could have been the energy of the date in hindsight, but I know good coffee.

His name was Heath (dreamy name BTW) and he was a great listener. It's interesting to reflect on that now, because it's one of the aspects about him that's always remained constant even in our currently mediocre marriage, but I'll get into that later. I probably talked too much, bitching and moaning about Chrissie, but he was good at feeling authentically invested. I wish I'd learned more about him, not to try and detect red flags or anything, but to even out the conversation.

Coffee turned into pre-lunch cocktails with a damn good cookie and I was suddenly very much wishing I wasn't here for such an intense obligation like your best friend's bachelorette party. I loved her, but I was feeling Heath. That's how fate works though doesn't it? Fate doesn't care about timing, only about its own agenda.

Sadly, and something I'll never forgive Chrissie for (as if we're friends still), my phone was obnoxiously blowing up. Even Kendall was looking for back-up.

It was time to go.

I gave a heavy sigh, but took matters into my own hands.

"I've really enjoyed this, Heath. And thanks for the drinks."

He waved it off. "No problem. I've enjoyed this too."

"Before I go off to see the devil…"

"You need me to anoint you with Holy Water?"

"Oh no, no. I get that done every other Tuesday, religiously." I joked back. "No, I was hoping I could get your number?"

I spotted the excitement in his eyes. There was a quick smile.

"Absolutely!" He recited the number while I recorded it and sent him a text. It's a safety measure to both test fake numbers, while also ensuring guys you really like know they have your number and don't ghost you like an asshole. After verifying that was not the case, I left in a dizzying swirl of caffeine and joy. Chrissie soon ruined that, but the rest of the weekend was fun, even if I could barely focus. And Steph put Chrissie in her place at one point, so that was a highlight.

Heath and I texted often in the following weeks, definitely an unhealthy amount. My intense focus on school was being slowly dismantled and I didn't care; my grades weren't suffering at all. If anything, I learned that I could reap the same rewards with less prep. It was a valuable life lesson to learn I could perform under pressure better than I'd thought. I slowly learned more about Heath too, like what he was going to school for and some of his background, which was quite sad. I got the sense that he was a bit of a recluse at college, not in a weird, serial-killer way, but just because he was totally comfortable with being alone. Whenever I'd ask what he was up to on the weekends it was usually, "Not much." Or "Studying. WBU?" I was still head over heels for the guy I'd only gotten coffee with thus far, but I noted it as a yellow-flag worth keeping an eye on.

Every once in a while, he'd kind of fall off the face of the earth. Never for more than a day, but I always wondered what he was up to, trying to not be that obsessive girl who cares about that stuff before we're even official. It was sporadic so I chalked it up to him just being busy.

After a month or so, I was starting to get bored and I was passing on other local guys for a purely virtual "relationship", if that's what you could call it. The coffee house and that first time he bumped into me was a distant memory, but in a moment of vulnerability he admitted similar thoughts and that he wanted to see me in person. Naturally, I suggested Denver because…well…Iowa City didn't sound exciting to me, at least not yet. I was even able to get my roommates to leave for the weekend which, in hindsight was presumptuous, but hey! I know what I want.

The first time he visited was a dream and all the energy and excitement around the relationship came flooding back. Within minutes of getting back to my apartment, we were fucking on the floor (sorry to be vulgar, but that's what it was) and the sex was crazy. Beyond the physical attraction that had been building, it was great to finally spend time with him. To remember and learn new quirks and mannerisms of one another. To share another meal together. Get a little drunk together. He asked me to be his girlfriend and I was smitten all over again.

I learned more about him, his passions, and his future, though arguably not as much as I wanted to. Heath was guarded about the finer details of what he wanted to do after school, which wasn't all that different from many of the other guys I'd met at DU. That was fine…even with my girlfriends, I'd learned not everyone has a five-year plan like I do. I've learned to recognize that my ambition is what sets me apart, not necessarily what I should hold others accountable to.

When Heath left, it hurt and I'd be lying if I said I wasn't afraid that our newly-cemented relationship wouldn't fizzle again. My worry ended up being unfounded - the story of my life sometimes - as we agreed I would book a trip to come visit him that next month. One trip turned into two, and that turned into a nearly monthly occurrence. Iowa City felt like Collegetown, USA and I had a blast each time. It was a far different environment than DU, but there was something invigorating about being on a busy, loud, and raucous college campus with Heath. Like I knew that someday we'd reflect on these moments as "the good ol' days" while our hair grayed.

I'd told my family about us and they were eager to meet him. I had to pump the brakes on that; I knew it would be a sensitive area for Heath and I didn't want to make him uncomfortable. At some point it would happen, but I wasn't about to rush it.

After several trips, there came a point where he called and said that he needed to go radio silent for a couple weeks. I could hear the anxiety in his voice, despite him trying to act unphased. He explained that it was a combination of a big project followed by a big test and he hadn't been doing well in the class thus far. I supported him and honored his wishes, but couldn't help but feel I was being lied to. I trusted him, but something felt…off. I was never able to put a finger on it and after those two weeks everything went back to normal, but it would happen several more times throughout our relationship. Big projects at work. Long travel trips. Surface level details suggesting I don't ask any more questions. I think he believes he was tricking me somehow…gaslighting me to not have interest in the "boring" details, but part of me always knew there was something else. Whatever *it* was, it didn't seem all that destructive and I left it alone. Maybe I shouldn't have, but the truth is I was narrowly focused on my own goals. At a certain point, I didn't have time to go weeding in other people's shit.

~~~

That goal was eventually achieved when I graduated with Honors from the University of Denver and was "recruited" by the FBI. I'm not sure if you could give them credit for recruiting me given that I'd been knocking on their door for the better part of a couple years, so we'll call it *strong mutual interest*. Despite that, the interview process was intense, and they even had to interview my family and close friends. I was still dating Heath at the time, but if I'm being honest, he kind of became second fiddle to the FBI gig when I first started. I'm not even sure he noticed at all because I'm able to juggle a bunch of balls well, but there were definitely times I was severely distracted. He eventually graduated too and got a job
~~~

on the international expansion team at a healthcare company, so I knew he was busy too.

I was able to station at the Denver FBI headquarters, starting off as an understudy, mentored by some of their better agents. I fit in with ease and my ambition was obvious to nearly everyone around me. One of my earliest mentors, Frank, applauded me for it, but also cautioned me.

"Not everyone likes ambition. Worse, but true, even fewer like an ambitious woman."

I remember we'd sat in silence a brief moment as he let the sentence linger. He continued.

"They can all go to hell. Just be careful who you bring with you - and who you overpass - along the way." He itched his thick mustache. "That make any sense?"

It absolutely did and I'd encountered shadows of it throughout my life already. "Completely. Thank you, Frank."

Given that I was in the Denver HQ, most of my early projects were drug related. Colorado wasn't a border state (to Mexico, that is), but was a major drug hub given how much the city was booming. Most of the time we supported local PD and investigatory units, but eventually we got to build a project team that had picked up details of drug and human trafficking across several states. They were some real nasty fuckers…the kind you never have a problem putting away. To make a long, very interesting story short, Frank and I spearheaded this special unit, codename "Gypsies", and through some very intense months, had enough damning material to raid seven separate installations simultaneously, arresting 25 high-ranking members, killing four others (not me, I wasn't in the field most of the time), and saving 50+ people from being trafficked, all while seizing nearly half a ton worth of drugs.

To say it was a huge win was an understatement, and it was around this time that Heath proposed, asking me to be his wife during a quick weekend trip we'd taken back to Austin. It was a chaotic but very happy period in my life and I was caught in a whirlwind of excitement. Excitement about my life with Heath. Excitement about where my career could go from here. Everything seemed to be looking up and I mean that it a non-ominous way…there was no "until…" that came after. I was crushing life.

Our wedding was small, largely because I knew Heath didn't have many friends or much family. It was a sensitive subject, even if he wouldn't admit it, so we kept the ceremony and reception quaint, but it was still a blast. In hindsight, I had zero time to plan any sort of huge wedding so it worked in that favor too. And I got my bachelorette party - Kendall and Steph joined - without any Chrissie in sight. (I'm a vindictive bitch, so sue me!)

~~~

Heath and I went on our honeymoon to the Amalfi Coast in Italy. As if I couldn't have fallen in love with him more, I did there. It was a moment in time of our relationship that I look back at us being fully connected. His distance and sometimes ambiguity was nowhere in sight, and I was a million miles away from work, absorbing the ocean breeze, pasta, pastries, bottles of wine, and those famous Italian lemons.

Our first afternoon after we'd recalibrated from jet lag, we were waking up from a wine-induced nap, having visited the beach earlier in the day. I awoke first and decided to surprise him with one of his honeymoon gifts: some new lingerie. Skin still crusted with sea salt, I slipped it on, freshened up a bit, and went back into the bedroom. By then, he was awake, scrolling on his phone without much purpose. The way his jaw dropped when he saw me could have broken the floor beneath.

"You like?" Was the best I could muster, even I knew the obvious answer.

"Um, yeah." His gaze had turned insatiable.

I wanted to tease him. "How about you ask me on one knee, like you did to propose."
~~~

He was sitting straight up in bed by now. "Oh, I'm not asking…"

That phrase, "I'm not asking…" became a common one in our relationship.

At times it was my favorite quirk phrase, reminding me of one of the happiest times in my life, and at others he could use it in mean ways. To talk down to me, or when we argued. Some "man of the house" type bullshit. That never sat well with me, but either way, "I'm not asking…" felt familiar to *us*.

Sometimes in marriages, it's the little stuff you pick up on the most.

~~~

Since our honeymoon, our marriage has stagnated to varying degrees. Or, at least, never been that high. We both went back to old habits; I got re-obsessed with work and Heath didn't…but remained elusive at times. Selfishly, I didn't need much from him because I had all the success and recognition I needed with my career. After the huge drug/human trafficking bust, I bounced around to some other projects as an advisor.

It was not only excellent and *damn* interesting experience, but it allowed me to make a name for myself within the Bureau as a whole, not just at the Denver headquarters. The phrase "everything under the sun" comes to mind in terms of what I encountered, and the job was ever changing and always interesting. The assholes Frank had warned me about were more present, especially on the East Coast for some reason, and I turned to him for guidance and mentorship on a frequent basis. And venting…quite a bit of venting.

That continued for several years and I'd been able to build a strong, efficient, and often innovative reputation within the FBI. Eventually that lent itself to my next big project which was a bit of a new foray for the agency. Stationed out of their Seattle HQ, and mostly "off the
~~~

books", they'd started gathering and profiling bank heists at an international level. Yep…good old-fashioned cops and robbers shit, all around the world. I almost couldn't believe it either; part of me thought the initial call was an elaborate prank.

When I went to the Seattle headquarters for the first time - located in the heart of the city - I was impressed with what the team had gathered, but even more so with the team itself. The heists were more elaborate than I'd suspected, which introduced an element of challenge that I craved. The team, looking for a strong leader, was ego-less (in a very good way), and very smart. Essentially not much more than a collection of analysts at the time, the amount of background research they'd been able to collect was impressive. Before the trip ended, I knew my answer was to take this role (it was a promotion, after all) and move to Seattle.

Heath was really happy for me when I told him. I'd had anxiety about the whole thing because I couldn't tell him the finer details outside of "It's a promotion, and it would require us to move to Seattle." Per usual, he didn't ask all that many questions anyway, but was more open to it than I'd suspected.

"I've never been to Seattle, but it sounds like we'll love it! The seafood and coffee alone have me excited." He hugged me and kissed my cheek. "It's also a pro-mo-tion! You're allowed to celebrate. You worked really hard for this."

"What about your work?" I asked to be supportive, but not *really* caring what the answer would be.

"I can work from anywhere. I'll still have to travel, but Seattle has a good international airport so I don't see any issue."

"Are we doing this?" I already knew the answer.

"Hell yeah we are!" We kissed again and once more, I felt close with my husband.

~~~
~~~

I could go on about how much we [mostly] loved Seattle (the rain sucks after a while) or how our marriage found brief new energy in this adventure and then quickly dissipated. But the heists and the work were so damn interesting, I was becoming obsessed in uncovering every single detail of various bank heists around the world. My team was too.

Sure, we had no jurisdiction in foreign lands - *technically* - but if we needed answers, or even an expenses-covered trip or two, I was able to make it happen. In total, we'd been following around 20 heists. Each was its own unique puzzle piece, some were more elaborate than others, and some were much larger scores than others. Our job was to profile all of them and find patterns. Were these one-off situations? Recurring hits? Skilled groups? Or "robbers for hire" being used one time?

The questions flowed fast and furious but all of them were anchored in our sole purpose: determining any patterns to *prevent* heists of these sizes on American soil in the future. Deep within me, I was slightly disappointed that it wasn't as powerful and heroic as saving human lives like I had with the trafficking project, but I knew there would be time to return to that later in my career. At the end of the day, the FBI needed me here and I couldn't deny how compulsively interesting it all was.

Over the course of a little over a year, we'd been able to draw connections between some of the heists. Almost disappointingly so, our running theory was that most of them were one-off situations. That didn't make them any less harmful, but it didn't help much with identification of patterns and potential "hot-spots". Several were linked together - including some very big ones - but there was one group in particular that I, or rather, *we*, became very intrigued by: **The Masks**.

They'd completed heists in Berlin, Naples, Austin, London, Malta, and most recently, Sydney. The Austin, Texas heist had particularly interesting as it seemed like they'd added someone new to their ranks and had been operating with four ever since. The Masks were enticing to study and borderline-revolutionary in their approach. Aside from their namesake, of which they always wore elaborate, fully covering masks, they operated by a clear set of rules. Their clothes were altered, to change the appearance of their bulk and height, and they never seemed to use the same tactics twice. Their cool-down time was significant, often more than two years in between, and they didn't aim all that high. They were talented and coordinated enough that my team and I believe they could have robbed some of the biggest banks in the world…yet they didn't. We guessed they had aggressive financial strategies with the stolen money, and were impressed they kept their egos in check. There was never any evidence found of them scoping out locales which was borderline impossible anyway because we had no idea what they looked like *and* they were likely leaving significant gaps of time between the research and heists.

Based on their profiling, we'd done the fun exercise of pulling data for any and all banks that would meet their criteria. The list was extensive, to say the least, so it was worth a good laugh, but one did catch my eye: in the heart of downtown Seattle, mere blocks away from FBI headquarters where we worked.

What're the chances, huh?

Part III
Similar Interests

"Ok everyone, gather here for a second." Bernard motions us to come to the center of the room - more like a fancy garage - that we're all working from. "How's everyone feeling?"

Jazz shrugs, Jasmine gives two sarcastic thumbs up but with a big smile. I nod.

"The quiet bunch. Ok then." He claps his thick hands. "We're a month out from the Seattle heist. There's still a lot to do, but I feel better about where we're at right now than I have with any one of our past heists.

"Recon has been complete for over six months, and this is clearly an easy mark. Let's review together, shall we?" Ever the showman, he brings out a small black clicker that dims the lights and starts a projector. You would have expected a chorus of moans, but we're professionals. We know that the more we repeat the plan, the more ingrained it will be.

"1301 5th Ave, Seattle. Code name: The Topple Building." We stare at a unique skyscraper; a long box of windows and metal, that sits precariously on top of a massive column of concrete that blossoms upward from the ground. Seattle has several unique buildings and skyscrapers, but I have always been surprised by this one. It feels like it borders on being unsafe, but the imagery is certainly effective.

"Our mark is on the ground floor on the east side of the building, along 5th Avenue. Sterling Bank of Seattle, or SBS for short. It's not part of a national chain, as we usually try to avoid those, but it's big enough to make it worth it. We also have solid intel that while this may be on the smaller scale of our heists, the several other SBS branches pool their money here before moving it to larger secure locations where we wouldn't have a chance at it.

"Based on their patterns, we believe the stock will be approximately 70-75% full before they'd transport it, meaning we're near the maximum amount of money we could expect that bank to ever have. Why not wait for the maximum? No ego amigo!"

"No ego amigo!" We all half-shout in unison. Rule #4.

"The great thing about this bank is its street location. University Street, half a block away, has a path straight toward I-5 north. From there, the interstate entrance is only two blocks and two stoplights away, including the left turn we'll need to make on University. Getting on the interstate should be quick and painless which only increases our chances of success, even if something goes awry. But it won't."

Bernard looks to me to takeover.

"Bernard's right. The location is optimal because of the proximity to the highway. We'll be in two separate vehicles: some inconspicuous, but fast, sedans. I'll drive one while Jazz takes the other. Bernard with me, Jasmine with Jazz. We'll review the getaway in a second. First, let's go through logistics."

Jazz, sitting spread legged in a classic black hoodie, has a raised hand.

"Yes, Jazz?"

"Sorry, Heath, but I have to mention this bit about the location as we should all be aware. It's the elephant in the room."

I've been worried about this, and Jazz is right. Might as well get it out of the way now.

"The Seattle FBI Headquarters is less than a quarter of a mile from the heist site. A 5-minute walk."

Of course, we each already know this, but it has been silently ignored until now. Jasmine shifts uncomfortably, crossing her legs the opposite of what they'd been. Bernard stares at a corner of the wall.

"Thank you, Jazz. It's something we should all know, but it doesn't change anything." No one argues, so I continue. "In fact, it could be in our favor. This is in their backyard; they'll never see it coming."

Bernard *tsk's* at that, but otherwise stays silent.

"I agree, Heath." Jasmine gives her vote of confidence. "I don't think it's that big of a deal. More a coincidence really."

"Spot on. The bank is a perfect mark for all the reasons we're careful about." Jazz adds.

I don't wait for Bernard to offer his support. It's there, unspoken. "Good, I'm glad we all feel that way. Now, let's dig into the specifics, shall we?"

~~~

I've just finished a hard-ass set of deadlifts and glance over to Heath. He is doing pull-ups slowly, with fantastic form. The muscles along his shoulders and upper back morph and flex as he drags himself upward. It is hot as fuck, but I'm still pissed at him. I put an additional 25 pounds on each side of the bar as anger therapy.

This morning he informed me of a business trip he has this upcoming week. Gone for nine days, which I always think is fucking weird…for his company to force him to travel over the weekend? But since it's international travel, there is no use for him to come back only to have to fly back out again. I am annoyed because apparently this trip has been planned for months, and he'd forgotten to tell me about it.

Of course, I don't have any *real* reason to be mad. We don't have a dog or kids or anything that I am suddenly strapped to find care-solutions for. But I will be alone, and it's just annoying as hell. If he knew this was on the calendar, why hadn't he told me? Is he really that forgetful? We'd rode
~~~

in silence to the gym on this Sunday morning because I don't have much to say to him.

Heath can be so distant sometimes.

So…disconnected. As if he doesn't give a shit about me.

It's frustrating. And when I'm angry or annoyed, I do deadlifts.

Plus, for some different stupid reason, work has been annoying me too. We've made it nowhere with any of the heist groups, including The Masks. They have been silent for a couple years by now, which is normal for them, I guess. Though something about our data pull was triggering for me.

A bank within nearly a stone's throw from our branch's headquarters.

Sterling Bank of Seattle.

I looked it up. It's in that weird building where the concrete structure holding the frame looks like a stiff breeze would send it tumbling down the steep Seattle streets.

Fuck it.

I finish my set of deadlifts. The weights slam. I usually hate people who do that.

I want to see what our data is telling us first hand. I'm going to go check out SBS this Tuesday morning, I'll have the extra time. We have no other leads, so what could it hurt?

~~~

Across the gym, I hear Laura slam her deadlifts while I rest between sets of pull-ups. Covertly, I peek up from my phone. A handful of people give her a similar glance and I know she feels strongly about when other people slam their weights. She must be really pissed, always keeping that shit contained…giving me the silent treatment.

Granted, I did fuck up. I got so caught up in the craziness of the Seattle heist that I completely forgot to create my "healthcare analyst" cover story, much less tell her about it. Frustratingly, I am torn.
~~~

On one hand, I feel sloppy with regards to my personal life which is *not* something I enjoy. The heist is in a good place - the plan is solid, tight, and well-rehearsed - but it doesn't count for shit if I fumble it with my FBI wife. Perhaps because this mission hits so close to home, I've been self-conscious this entire time, forcing my mind to forget this element. Jazz's callout triggered an "Oh shit!" moment that I should have acted on sooner.

Then, on the other hand, I want to tell Laura to calm the fuck down. So she has to watch Netflix or work late by herself for a few nights? It's not like we live these posh, busy lives. We're boring. Now she's just forced to be boring alone. What's the big fucking deal?

Per usual, my guilt overrides my ability to care about those questions. Truth is: I fucked up and maybe there's a way I can say sorry in a nice way. Our friends recently told us about a downtown restaurant they loved, Purple, that doubles as a wine bar. Apparently, the staff is super knowledgeable about wine and it has fantastic food with a cool aesthetic. That it's only a couple blocks away from the heist location so I can get a quick scan is just an added benefit.

You're playing with fire Bernard's voice bounces around in my head. I shake it off and get back to my workout. In between my next few sets, I am surprisingly able to reserve a table that evening. Now it's just a matter of if Laura wants to actually go. Done with deadlifts, she is walking toward a machine near me. I try to catch her gaze while smiling, but she ignores me.

A million miles away on purpose.

Her car door shuts - or rather *slams* - as we leave the gym to go back home. Immediately, she gets her phone out and begins mindlessly scrolling.

Ok…guess I'll be starting this conversation.

"I have a surprise." I start.

"Another work trip?" She bites back. I wince slightly but let it go.

"No…something to make up for being so forgetful about this week's trip." The lead-in is met with total silence. "I made us a reservation tonight."

"So a fancy dinner? That's the guilt acting."

I flip my blinker and turn onto a new street.

"C'mon Laura." I deliver it with a mix of frustration and remorse. It seems to work.

"Ugh! Fine. I'm still pissed though so I'm getting a super nice wine."

"Fair enough." I smile.

"And dessert."

I laugh. "We'll see!"

"Oh, I'm not asking." She mocks.

"Ok, ok. And dessert then."

And just like that, we're back to normal. I think…

~~~

Purple was a truly delicious dinner, and even better wine. Damn Heath for burying the hatchet so easily, but I'll be fine I suppose. It's a long work trip, but I'm slammed with my own work right now and it won't change my routine much. I'll just miss him…or having someone around more accurately.

I twitch at that thought while I take a heavy swig of rich, burgundy wine.

Has our relationship fizzled so much that I don't actually miss him, but just like having a body around?

"Hey," Heath is across the table studying me. "Where are you?"

"Hmm?" I blink a couple times and pull my thoughts back to the table. The wine's sweetness lingers on my tongue. "Sorry, was off in la la land."

"Yeah, well…" He's smiling, twirling a spoon. "You better come back before I finish this entire dessert."
~~~

I stare down at the crème brûlée, gorgeously crusted with torched sugar and adorned with two plump blackberries. It's nearly half gone.

"What the hell?" I grab my spoon and immediately dive in. Like hell I'm letting him eat my whole dessert.

Heath laughs and leans back in his seat, arms raised in faux surrender. Our waiter comes by silently and fills up our glasses with the remainder of the bottle resting on the table.

"Anything else I can get you folks this evening?"

"Probably just the check?" Heath looks to me for approval. I nod in agreement, mouth full of crème brûlée and a blackberry.

"Absolutely." The waiter darts off.

"I'm hoping this was a good apology?" Heath prods. "I'm sorry again for forgetting about my work trip."

"Yes," I smile. "This is a great apology. And it's fine. I'm sorry too. I was being dramatic about the whole thing. I'll be fine. Work is crazy anyway so between that and the gym, it'll fly by."

"Ok. What are you working on these days anyway? What's the FBI got cookin?" He jokes.

"Well, per usual, I can't tell you certain things, but you know how we moved here for that big project?"

He nods. *Obviously he knows, Laura.*

"It has kind of stalled out. We have a ton of data to comb through and my analysts are amazing, but finding the patterns has been difficult. Strangely, we're in a waiting pattern right now until something else happens. Plenty of research to be done day-to-day still, but I don't know. I wish it were going better." That's the most I've talked about my job with him in a while.

"Hmmm. Well aside from that being the vaguest update I've ever heard; it sounds like you need to shake things up. Just my two cents, fully understanding I have no idea what I'm talking about."

"What do you mean?"

"You've hit a wall. Sometimes the best thing to get around that wall is doing something different. Walk away and focus elsewhere, follow hunches instead of logic…stuff like that."

"Hmmm." I think about it while I take my final sip of wine. The waiter drops the check off without saying a word, not wanting to bother us. "You may be right…Thanks."

I feel like I should ask about his job. About his work trip. I know I'll get equally vague answers.

The secrets we keep.

Heath prevents me from doing so. "You ready?" He stands and grabs his coat.

We push through the massive metal door at the front of the restaurant, onto the street. It's chilly, but not as biting as I would have expected. *Probably the wine.*

My office is only a block or so away.

So is the bank. I want to check it out and see if I notice anything…unique. I've been second-guessing my choice to go visit it ever since the gym. *It's just a stupid hunch.*

Shake things up…Heath's advice didn't fall on deaf ears. It bounces around in my mind.

"C'mon. We can go this way to the car." I take his hand, fibbing a bit. Technically it'll be an extra block, but he won't notice. The bank is close, less than a three-minute walk. Nonchalantly, we stroll past it, sitting on the ground floor of the building that looks like it might fall over. It's more open than I would have expected (and from what I can see with the lights off), but the entire street-facing, front side is glass. I quickly note the I-5 directional signs.

Hmm. That would be a fast getaway.

I'm convinced enough by what I mentally gather in these ten seconds that I want to come back when they're open. Assess the interior. The traffic patterns. Talk with the staff.

It's settled then.

~ ~ ~

My heart is beating the shit out of the inside of my chest. Bernard screams in my brain: *You shouldn't be doing this! What the fuck are you doing, kid?*

He's right. I'm not sure why Laura walked me this way to go to our car. She *led* me here.

Even my idea about scouting the bank one last time was a dumb one, much less the fact that I was *following* her.

Does she know? How the fuck would she know?

I try to act as normal as possible without overdoing it. There are likely cameras around and this footage will be combed through extensively after the heist. I can't risk creating any suspicion.

Since I'm here, I use my peripherals to glance around, looking for things that may be different than what our intel has told us. Nothing piques my interest, but I do wish we could pull off the heist at night, once the bank is closed. It's almost deserted in this part of town on a Sunday evening. That's not the plan though, and a quick shift to that time frame would be too risky. Not to mention, Jazz has assured us the response time to alarms is slower during the day and we need a manager to access the vault quickly. Doing it without one would take nearly an hour, and I trust his research. He's yet to be wrong.

Laura's hand feels icy in mine, probably because mine is clammy.

My nerves remain on edge. She glances around briefly, like a breeze through the buildings.

I have to wonder if she can hear my heart toddler-pounding on my ribs as we walk to the car and drive home.

I leave for my "work" trip early the next morning. In reality, I only travel further outside of downtown, deeper into the woods of the Pacific Northwest. We are two hours outside of Seattle, in a cabin surrounded by thick trees. It is some family's second home and Bernard has paid a sizable amount of money under the guise we are on a company retreat. Eagerly, the family accepted and were paid from an account the Advisor assures us is untraceable.

Halfway through the day, Jazz and I each drive to an old, dilapidated parking lot that is full of old cars. More a junkyard than a place many used for active parking, it will be the perfect place to swap out vehicles directly after the heist. We'll reduce from the two sedans used during the heist to a single SUV. Here, there's no cameras, it's still close to the freeway, and has minimal traffic. From there, we'll drive into Montana and stay at another cabin under the same "business trip" moniker. Our route is completely mapped out to avoid areas of consistent police coverage and reduce the number of times we are caught on camera. Along the way, we'll swap license plates three times and refuel from extra gas canisters, meaning that by the time we arrive in Montana, we should be ghosts.

"You nervous?" Jazz asks in his Australian accent as he drives. He opted for a slightly brighter hoodie color today: gray.

"I guess. A little. The plan feels tight though. You?" I answer. We are driving back from dropping off the getaway SUV. Out the window, the skies are cold and full of low clouds.

"Oh of course. I always get really bad the days before a heist."

"Really? I've never noticed."

"'T's mostly internal stuff. Anxiety. Stuff like that, mate." He pauses and I wonder if he has shared this with the rest of the crew before. Probably only Jasmine. "Day-of though, it's go-time. My adrenaline runs so high that it's like my anxiety never happened. Weirdest thing."

"Are you okay right now?"

"Hmm? Oh yeah. Just nervous as fuck, ya know. Every heist is a huge risk. You think about it…today could be our last day as free people. Are you doing what you'd want to on your last free day? I know I'm not, but that's the game."

Damn. I'd never thought of it that way before.

Tuesday morning. Early.

That Tuesday morning.

We all woke up early, had some coffee and Jasmine's syrup concoction, but otherwise were too nervous to eat.

Now we're in our two different sedans, only blocks away from the Sterling Bank of Seattle along 5th Ave. Moments away from starting the heist.

Jazz's comments tumble around my thoughts as I mindlessly navigate the downtown Seattle streets. There're other cars scattered around, but traffic is light because it's only 5 AM. Bernard sits beside me, silent as usual. I try to make some conversation about strategy,

"Have we ever wondered if people could get a good look at us through the car windows?"

"Yep. Jazz has installed a special film on all our vehicles' windows for the past several heists. Reflective tinting essentially, without being attention grabbing. He's never told you that?"

"I guess not." I reply, learning the detail for the first time. Bernard, similarly nervous, keeps the discussion going.

"These masks Jasmine made are next level." In his hand is an eerie, golden face…that of a Greek god. "Zeus. King of the Gods."

"There some sort of metaphor behind that?" I ask

Bernard gruffs his reply. "I'm not sure, but they're creepy as fuck. I love 'em."

We return to silence as I pull the car to the side of the road, keeping it running. Behind me, I see the distinct headlights of Jazz and Jasmine's vehicle.

The vehicles are a block away and it's here we'll stay until the manager arrives. Bernard speaks into an earpiece.

"20 minutes everyone. Manager usually gets here around 5:20. Lay low, check your gear, get your shit together."

"Copy." - Jasmine

"Copy." - Jazz

"Copy." I state, the final mark for the group before we go.

Time to steal some money…

Part IV

Just Another Tuesday Morning

5:29 AM
Only a handful of vehicles have passed us this early morning, but there's a mild increase to the overall stream. It's cold out, having rained last night. Even inside the car, petrichor's iconic scent is noticeable. Strangely, we'd not had much rain over the last week.

By citing the weather, you'd think I'm calm. Relaxed.

Truth is, my nerves are frazzled. For the last 10 minutes I've been running through my Sunday night date with Laura, when she walked us past the bank that's merely a block ahead of me right now. Almost as if she was taunting me.

Does she know?

Does the FBI?

Is this a massive sting operation?

My mind runs away with worst-case scenarios until I hear a voice in my ear.

"Manager is in. Handful of employees too. Single security guard." Jazz lets us know what the cameras inside are seeing.

"Mask up, people." Bernard barks across the channel. "Check comms once your mask is on."

Two "checks" come from the other car and Bernard and I echo. The voices sound different because of the modulators built into the mask.

"Everyone make sure there're no facial features or hair showing. Tuck the mask's hood into your shirts." Jasmine explains. "Can everyone breathe ok? Can everyone see ok?"

I take some deep breaths through the material, surprised that it feels as if it isn't there. Aside from a mild screen-like haze in my vision, I can see fine too. Jasmine has outdone herself with these.

"Just fine, Jasmine." Bernard replies.

I follow. "These are incredible, nice job." My modulated voice sounds deep, partly robotic.

"Thanks." Hers doesn't sound feminine at all.

Bernard provides the next instructions. "Check weapons. Live ammo, safeties on to start." He pauses a moment. "Okay. When we pull up, this is live. Focus. We're a team, we leave as a team. If we encounter resistance, no killing. Aim for non-lethal shots if it absolutely comes to that."

"Cars on our left. Wait." Jazz states, mild as can be. A stream of three pedestrian cars passes ours, continuing in the direction of the bank ahead. Bass pumps through the speaker system of one, fading quickly. I wait for the phrase that will start the whole thing.

All clear.

"All clear." Jazz speaks.

I tap the gas and guide the car forward until the bank is immediately on the right.

Bernard growls. "Go time."

He's out the door before I even have it in park. I'm swift to follow, leaving the car running, locked until I return with the key fob in close enough proximity.

Jazz and Jasmine pull up behind us, repeating the motions. Soon enough, we're in a square formation, walking briskly with weapons down, toward an employee entrance on the right-hand side of the building. The extra steps will provide us an entrance that sets us up more strategically inside, but we'll still exit out the bank's main doors toward the parked vehicles. Thus far, we've not seen other people which is good; the masks and heavy weaponry would surely elicit a reaction.

As we move toward the entrance, I get reacquainted with my altered gait. Courtesy of some smart shoe designs by

Jasmine, I appear two inches taller than I really am, with a "limp" on my left side. All of us have various physical attributes built falsely into our wardrobe to throw off any investigations, forcing their focus on details that aren't real.

"Heath on door." Bernard states quietly. He goes to the left side of the entrance while Jasmine and Jazz press against its right. Jazz checks a screen on his wrist and nods.

"You're good."

Gently, I press downward on the handle, pushing the door inward. A small moan escapes its hinges, but I press harder, transitioning into the building, and the noise stops. The other three follow behind, Bernard catching the door before it latches, closing it inaudibly. We're in and no one's the wiser. There will be no camera footage as Jazz took recordings from a couple weeks ago, splicing them over today's.

So far so smooth.

Now that we're a couple minutes into this operation, my nerves have settled. If the FBI were here, they'd have been waiting for us upon entry. Right?

The room we've entered is a hallway that leads to an employee break room. To our right is a dark office; the bank manager's when she's not out on the floor. It's a drearily dull hallway, with fluorescent lighting, thin, hard carpet, and several aged papers and fliers hanging from corkboards along the wall. Even through the mask it smells stale and it's clear the employees haven't come back here yet to put away their lunches or make a pot of crappy coffee.

Better for us.

We hear laughter outside the room, coming from the main atrium.

"Push in. Let me do the talking to start. Otherwise, you know the script." Bernard recites. "Ready zipties, we'll be going in peaceful. Let's keep it that way."

I lead us through the hallway, our footsteps only mild squishes on the floor. We turn through a short L-shaped corridor, emerging into the bank's main lobby. It's a far cry from the clichéd break room…there are literally red-carpet walkways along shiny brown and cream marble tile. Large columns of concrete - part of the "Topple" building's structure - go from the floor all the way to high ceilings. From our review of the layout, we know there's this main section, where many of the bankers' desks sit in an open configuration, along with a long teller counter. Across the atrium is a side portion of the lobby that extends into an oddly long hallway leading to guest bathrooms, other parts of the overall building, and an additional entrance to the teller counter, where the safe is located.

I shift my weapon to the ready, pressed against my inner shoulder. Safety on.

A female employee, her face still elated with the final flexes of laughter, looks in my direction. The high eyebrows and smile transform into higher eyebrows and a near-scream. Her co-workers, including the manager, notice and follow her gaze. I bring a "shh" finger in front of the mask, an act where the creepiness of the gesture is not lost on me.

Bernard addresses the group before they can speak, lowering his gun to build trust and reduce himself as a threat.

"Everyone stay calm. We are not here to hurt anyone." The words ring a bit hollow through the mask and voice modulation. "I know it doesn't look or sound like it, but I very much want all of you to get home to your families tonight. That, along with conducting a robbery, is our primary goal today."

Jazz and Jasmine are pointing their guns upward, searching windows and other viewpoints for initial threats. We already know there should be none, but in case you haven't noticed yet, we're the most careful bank robbers on the planet.

Bernard continues. "First order of business," he points to the security officer. "Sir, if you'd please lay your gun on the ground. One of my colleagues will come retrieve it, zip tie your wrists, and take your radio. Are there any other security officers present right now?"

Across the room, the rigid, portly man is thinking. Slowly, he removes his gun, unclips the radio, and shakes his head to Bernard's question. The intensity in the air dials down several notches and Jazz walks over to follow through on instructions.

"Good, thank you. You're doing great folks." He encourages. "Next up: who's the manager?"

We already know the answer, but this is a good test of their willingness to cooperate.

In the center of the group, a woman with copper, frizzled, shoulder-length hair, wearing a fitted teal blazer steps forward. Her name plate reads: "Tiffani". I expect a shake in her voice, but there is none,

"I am." It is actually her.

"Wonderful. We'll be putting everyone else in zipties, and I'd like them huddled over here, out of sight from the entrance." He points at a wall close to us while Jasmine joins Jazz to restrict wrists. I anchor my stance, gun pointed at the civilian group, studying any would-be heroes hidden among them. Because we are so early, it's a light group thus far, just a single male and a single female outside of the manager and security officer, neither of which look threatening. If anything, they are far more fearful than they should be, the male quivering.

I ask a question, "When should we expect the next employees to arrive?" It's another answer we know, but that we'd rather double check. The manager replies, turning to me. She looks cautiously angry. *She's a brave one.*

"We run light in the morning. This will be it until 10."

Bernard nods and takes back over. "Thank you. You all are doing great. Let's get started and I must urge you to not attempt anything. No calls outward, no emergency buttons, no running for the exits or fighting back. This will be over quickly and as I stated earlier: our secondary goal is to leave you completely unscathed. That changes if you put our primary financial objective at risk."

I begin to wonder if the masks are too effective because there's something even *creepier* about the kill-them-with-kindness routine stemming from the immovable, golden Zeus mouth.

"Let's just get this over with." The manager states while Jazz and Jasmine guide the group toward the wall near the breakroom where we entered.

"Very well." Bernard replies. "What's the easiest way to the vault?"

The manager's reddish curled hair bounces as she doesn't reply, turns on a heel, and walks toward the opposite hallway. Bernard follows, commenting as he passes. "Stay out of sight from the glass as much as possible. In three minutes, come back and help me pack."

There's a loud, extended beep - the side teller door unlocking with the manager's keycard - and she pokes out from behind the concrete side of the hallway.

"You coming?" She questions, annoyed.

Bernard hustles toward her, disappearing behind the corner.

I relax my shoulders. *We're well on our way.*
This is going smoothly.

~~~

I slept fucking awful last night, despite my wide-open bed. With Heath not there, I was starfishing hard, but once the early morning hours rolled around, I couldn't get back to sleep.

For some reason, I'm anxious about visiting this bank today.

SBS, Sterling Bank of Seattle. Very near our headquarters and one of the *many* banks that popped on our analytical attempt to narrow in on The Masks' type of bank they go after.

It's one of hundreds, but still…
~~~

I almost went to the gym to get my mind off things, but I figure I'll go there afterwards and take the day working from home, hopefully getting a nap once my nerves calm down. There's nothing I expect to find other than it being a perfectly normal building that just so happens to hold other peoples' money. Rolling over, the clock across the room beams red numbers: 4:30 AM.

Instinctively, I reach for my phone and mess around on it for ten minutes, deciding in the process that I'll get showered, dressed, and head to the bank early. They open at 6:45 AM - early for a bank, and part of the criteria that made it appear in the data - so I imagine there could be employees there at 5:40ish. I plan on flashing my badge, talking to a manager, sans any customer interruptions, getting a cup of coffee, and being at the gym before 8, easily. A productive morning that I'm not sure will tell me anything, but my curiosity is getting the better of me right now.

As I roll out of bed from underneath the warm covers, I remember I haven't told my team and question myself if I should do so. I hesitate out of embarrassment. *They'll think I'm crazy, chasing a 1 in 700 lead. And that's assuming our algorithm is precise.* I decide to keep it to myself and I'll tell them if anything interesting comes from it.

Mindlessly, I've been getting ready for the shower, and as I step into the warm stream, a semi-depressing thought reiterates itself:

This trip will lead to nothing; it's the perfectionist in me.

The rest of my routine was nothing special and my drive into downtown was similarly uneventful, though I have to say: I fucking love it when there's light traffic. I'm able to make it to the bank within 20 minutes and I park across the street from the entrance Heath and I walked by on Sunday night. Briefly, I wonder how his work trip is going…probably boring. When he gets back, I should ask him for once…

A pair of vehicles parked in front of the bank catch my eye for odd reasons: they're identical, gray Dodge Chargers, both with heavily tinted windows, and they seem to be idling. Their headlights and taillights are all off, but the smallest trail of exhaust is visible in the brisk morning air. *Odd…*

I can't imagine why they're parked there and pay no mind aside from the mental note I've already jotted down. Before exiting my own vehicle, I double check for my phone, my gun (holstered), and my badge. I review my minimal makeup in the rear-view mirror, wipe a quick smudge from underneath my left eye, and get out, locking my car. It delightfully responds with two "beeps" as I stride across the street.

I pass in front of the Charger sedans - sure as shit, they're still running - and don't see anybody inside them. Even through the heavy tint, there's no shapes or outlines of anyone.

"Ok, weird…" I mumble. The very edge of my instincts tingle, like the end of a string blowing in a breeze. My steps slow and I alter my approach to the front door, angling so that I'm not fully in front of any glass windows. *Am I crazy? What's going on here?*

Along the massive glass panels, there are dropped shades from closing time the previous evening. They are my guide, my map, to avoid detection until I can tell what the fuck is going on. My head screams at me that I'm being illogical, but down in my gut and chest, there's a gentle tightness…something reassuring that's urging caution. I've learned to listen to it.

Peering through the shades, I'm not able to gather much other than shapes. There are people inside for sure, mostly just standing about, but it's not obvious what they're doing or who they are. I try to think of logical reasons for the parked, empty, idling cars that have been left behind me. Not many come to mind, but I also struggle to narrow in on what "worst case scenario" is here.

A bank heist? That would be rich.

My glacial pace along the glass, crouched and probably looking like a crazy person, finally arrives to a panel without drawn shades. With a similar speed, I spy into the main lobby, ornate with red carpeting, fancy tiling and furniture, and ugly concrete pillars that support the main building. A tall man stands 20 feet further inside, wearing all black. It takes me a moment to register the next few things as the tightness in my gut becomes an outright boa constrictor.

He has a black hood of some sort.

He's holding a weapon. A rifle, but I can't tell which kind.

Unaware of my presence, his head turns, partially, mostly, toward me.

An elaborate gold mask…of some Roman or Greek person.

Without thinking, I duck completely down, resting a knee on the concrete, keeping my back flat and head out of sight. My hand goes to my gun.

Holy fucking shit.

"Holy fucking shit." I repeat aloud. My thoughts race and my heart boxes with my ribcage as its opponent.

The Masks.

The chances of this are astronomical. Impossible. Should I call someone?

My team? *What are they going to do?*

Backup? *Probably, but when would they get here?*

Heath? *Why the fuck would you do that right now?*

Hastily, I pull out my phone and send a succinct text to an FBI line we're supposed to use in case of emergency.

> "Bank robbery, on site
> Seattle, 5th Avenue
> SBS Bank"

There won't be any reply for security reasons, but I know it's been received. Now I must make the decision to wait or stop this myself. I'm frightened, but I've studied The Masks enough to know they avoid violence at all costs. They've never killed anyone, so I highly doubt an FBI agent would be their first.

Plus, I'm stubborn as hell and this would be a career game-changer.

You got this, Laura.

Only a handful of cars have passed on 5th Avenue in recent moments, and there have been no pedestrians. I'm mildly grateful for the early morning timing so that - if anything - the collateral damage will be minimal. Of course, they planned it that way.

Slowly, I remove my gun from its holster and stretch my hamstrings; they've been on fire while crouching. Despite that, I remain as low as possible, and peek inside one last time. The man in the lobby remains in place, facing away from the front. I take that advantage to study other elements of the bank's interior. On my right, against a far wall, I spot another Mask, as well as some civilians sitting against said wall. My angle isn't perfect but I can see another pair of legs stretched out…I have to assume there are a handful of hostages and at least two more Masks, one of which would be in the vault.

Once I've noted all I can, I slink along the front of the building, heading toward its left side. I turn right, intentionally looking for an emergency exit along a hallway I spotted. It's on the opposite side of the hostages and is secluded enough that it'll allow me to get inside and have an element of surprise.

Unless, of course, they have someone on THAT door.

"Chill out, Laura." I threaten myself as I lean against the corner and cautiously peek around it.

Nothing.

Windows are sparse along this edge so I haul ass along the length of the building, quickly arriving at a nondescript steel door. The gleaming silver handle doesn't budge, unsurprising, but there's a keypad next to it, with 12 slightly worn buttons. It's a brand I'm familiar with, and I use my phone to remotely access the FBI database. Every keypad manufactured after a certain date has an emergency reset path that law enforcement (or the owner) can use to gain access in a crisis.

Within minutes, I have this brand and model pulled up and meticulously follow the steps to initiating the reset.

Hold " # " and " * " for 3 seconds.

Wait for a beep.

Hold " # " and " * " for another 3 seconds.

Wait for 2 beeps.

Type code: " #*##0*7#3* "

Wait for a final beep.

The chime tells me I've completed the sequence so I test the handle once more, hoping I didn't screw up the process. It presses down and I've got access.

With a deep breath, I move through its threshold, striving to not make a sound.

Immediately, the vastness of the space chills me; I'm insanely exposed in this hallway.

Even worse, there's a Mask on their way, turning toward me from watching the hostages across the room.

He (she?) must be headed to the vault to assist with the money packing.

It's now or never, Laura.

"Put your hands in the air!" I yell, wondering if I should have gone with a whisper instead. Too late now.

Across the room, there's a small scream from a hostage. In my peripherals, I sense two Masks closer to them, reacting to my voice's direction. The Mask directly before me - taller than them - wheels on a single heel, the deep darkness of his barrel staring me down. I half expect the motion to come coupled with a bullet, but he restrains himself…instead seeming taken aback.

I shout with more authority this time. "I said, put your fucking hands in the air!" By now, sunlight has started to penetrate the small slits of the eastern blinds. The man - I'm sure it's a man now, just by how he carries himself - is frozen. The golden, frightening mask of some Greek god of old peers at me with black eyes. Sweat beads under my armpits and a flash of heat presses along my brow. Behind him, the other Masks are controlled chaos, knowing something has gone sideways, but remaining confident and focused on their jobs.

Perhaps reasoning with him could help?

"Look man, drop the gun. You haven't done too much wrong so far. You can come out of this with your life still intact. I just need you to put down your gun and put your hands in the air. Slowly."

Finally, he responds with a heavily altered, mechanical voice. "I'm not going to put my gun on the floor." Hearing words come through the motionless mouth of the mask stands my hair on end. "I will, *slowly*, slide my gun to my back and raise my hands."

Without thinking, I respond. "That's not good enough. Gun on the floor."

"I'm not asking…" *That fucking phrase, the same my husband uses.* "So what happens now, miss…?"

"My name is Laura. What happens now is that you tell your boys to stop piling cash away, we wait for my backup, while you remove the mask and lay on the ground." I allow the instructions to sink in. "If all of that goes smoothly, you *might be* out of jail in less than five years' time."

His reply is immediate. "And if it doesn't? Go smoothly, that is?"

An eerie morning silence permeates across the entire bank floor upon this challenge.

"I will shoot you. And then it's anyone's game. But I promise you, I'm a good enough shot that you will not walk away from it." I add a bluff for emphasis. "I really don't want to kill anyone today, but I have before. Don't test it."

That may have worked…he shifts briefly side to side before speaking again.

"I don't want you to shoot me either, but we're not going to do any of what you're asking. I offer another route: you sit down with the other hostages - none of whom will come to any harm - let us go about our business, and we all move on with our lives. Alive and not in jail."

Does this guy think I'm just going to fucking roll over and die?

"You know I can't do that and my patience is wearing thin." Heat blossoms across my brow and chest anew. I readjust my grip around the firearm; it has weighed heavy during this interaction. "Take the fucking mask off, now. I'm not asking…"

Heath would be proud of that usage.

It is my last thought before a heavy bludgeon to the side of my head turns my world black.

~~~

"…I'm not asking…" Laura states with a scowl and a very real intent to use her weapon. Thank God for these masks because beneath mine, I'm riddled with anxiety, fear, and confusion. More immediately however, is concern.

In my peripheral, Bernard has emerged from the doorway that leads to the bank teller stations and vault. Laura can't see him and he holds a single "quiet" finger in front of the terrifying mouth of Zeus. The tension of my worlds colliding together is almost too much to bear. Deep within, I want to call out to Bernard, tell him to wait, remove my mask, and escape all this before it's too late.

But that's just the thing…

It's already too late.

We're in the middle of a heist. I have to play the role.

Laura's eyes are glowering. She'll shoot me if I make any movements.

Behind her, Bernard raises the butt of his weapon slowly, methodically.

He brings it down hard on the side of her skull and I watch her eyes immediately roll back. She ragdoll-falls to the granite tiling hard and I run to check her pulse. There's a surge of anger at Bernard, but I know there were very few
~~~

other options. He stands for a moment as I tend to my wife, remembering that I can't *overdo* it. The hostages are watching and I shouldn't give the slightest hint that I know this woman.

"She good?" Bernard asks. I catch a strong undercurrent of frustration.

"She'll be fine." I respond, noticing a thin trail of blood tricking down the side of her head, along her cheek.

"Good. Let's get this shit moving." He snaps his fingers and whistles toward Jazz and Jasmine. "One of you come here and take her over to the other hostages." Then he addresses the frightened people themselves, "You see what happens? I could have SHOT her! Let's all pay attention and you'll be okay. I will not have as much mercy with the next hero."

He's definitely angry and walks closer to me. Jazz has since made his way over as well.

"Leave her. Get in back with me and the vault. We need to speed this up big time." As he starts walking away, he adds, "Thanks to you."

I knew I wasn't going to get an apology from him for smiting my wife across the head, but I certainly didn't think I'd receive blame either.

How the fuck was I supposed to know she'd be here?

I'm deathly silent, avoiding Bernard's temper and running a thousand scenarios through my mind of how I may have slipped up. None come immediately to memory and my conscience scolds me.

Focus, Heath. You may have fucked up, but you're in the middle of a heist right now. Here *it means life or death.*

I've been mindlessly following Bernard along the path toward the vault, centrally located behind the teller counter.

"Tiffani?" Bernard questions, searching for the frizzle-haired manager.

Nothing.

We come around to the front of the vault and it's closed. Tiffani is nowhere in sight.

"Had you opened the vault yet?"

"She was supposed to while I was checking on you." The reply was huffy. I didn't need to say anything, he knew he shouldn't have left a hostage unattended. "Fuck! Where is she?"

"Do you think she ran away?" My question causes Bernard to jog around the vault and along the outer walls of this back room.

"I don't see how she could have. All of the exits would have had our eyes on them. There's no way out from back here."

Through our Zeus' eye slits, our gaze connects, and simultaneously turns toward the vault door.

"She locked herself in there." I state.

"Shit."

"Can anyone else access it?" I already know the answer. Bernard does too, and takes me by the shoulder to a corner of the room.

He whispers in low tones, "She's the only one here that can get into that vault. We need to make a decision fast."

"What choice do we have? We should take what we can from the front registers and go. It'll probably be a few thousand, but otherwise this job is busted."

"I wonder why that is?" Bernard bites back.

"Look, I have no fucking idea how she's here, but there's no use in it right now. Solve the fucking problem." I scold him and his childish anger. "Focus up." He knows I'm right.

"We have another option." There's a darkness in his voice. "We could create some leverage." I watch as he turns off the safety of his weapon.

"Bernard...no."

"Why not?"

"What're you going to do? Kill somebody? What about our rules?"

"I'm not killing anyone. Injuring maybe. We can get her to think we will unless she comes out."

"I don't like it. Jazz and Jasmine won't either."

We both know we won't singlehandedly win this argument. Without another word, we hustle over to the front teller counter corner closest to the side where Jazz and Jasmine are holding the hostages. Bernard gives a slick and short whistle that catches their attention. Jasmine strolls over facing us while Jazz walks backward, weapon loosely pointed at the hostages. Most of them are remarkably calm, only their glistening eyes betraying their attempts to hide their fear.

"What's up?" She asks. The voice modulator makes her sound more like a man. Jazz leans in, only listening.

"The manager locked herself in the vault. We're running out of time." Bernard starts, talking as softly as possible. "We have two options. Option #1: we take the money from the cash registers along this counter and leave within two minutes. Option #2: we take a hostage, bring them back here, and apply some pressure for her to open the vault. Either way, we need to be gone in ten minutes, preferably sooner."

"Is this a vote?" Jasmine inquired.

Bernard's reply was terse. "Sure."

"I vote #2. Didn't come here for chump change." Jazz states quickly.

"I vote for both." Jasmine answers. "He [motioning toward Jazz] can watch the other hostages, I can empty these registers, and you two can try and get in the vault. At seven minutes we get the fuck out of dodge."

"What the hell happened to 'no ego amigo'?" I counter. "This job is busted. We need to get out of here ASAP."

The group remains quiet and suddenly I feel like "the new guy" all over again, even though it's been many years since that has been true. Jasmine is the first to respond,

"Babe," She avoids using my real name. "You know I love you, but this is your fault. It sucks, but somehow, someway, that's at least partially true. Based on our other rules we'll be without this score for *at least* two years. This is a measured response…a calculated risk."

"It's settled then." Bernard takes over. "Watch the hostages [he points to Jazz], you clean out these registers [Jasmine nods at her instructions], and you [he means me] go meet me by the vault. I'll pick a hostage."

I'm at a loss for words. My chest is tightening and this grandiose bank entrance suddenly feels claustrophobic. I know we should get out of here. We shouldn't be doing this. We should know when to take the loss.

Am I overly against this right now because my wife is lying unconscious nearby?

There's a scream of terror as Bernard grabs a hostage. There's pleading coming from a male voice and I know immediately who Bernard chose: the one who was quivering as we ziptied their wrists. Though I'm against this idea, it's the smart move taking the person who will be the most dramatic. The more we can get him to play into our hand - and think he's about to die - the more likely we can get the manager out of the vault.

Bernard lets him continue to whimper as he rounds the corner, through the side doorway, dragging him by the arm. Once he sees there are two of us, the panic sets in even more. Tears stream down his red, flushed cheeks. Slobber and snot are draining from his nose and he looks a mess.

Good God. Have some dignity.

"Please, *please!* I'll do anything! What do you want?"

This sort of dramatic pleading continues in between sobs. By now, he has fallen to his knees. Bernard and I continue to ignore him while I hear Jasmine behind us rushing from register to register packing away all the money within. Beside me, Bernard moves various pieces of his rifle, being sure to make as much threatening noise as possible. I nearly laugh because he's actually not doing anything of consequence, but the whimpering fool in front of us doesn't know any better.

"Oh GAWD! I'm going to die." His shivering is violent now…uncontrollable. There's a soft pitter-patter sound as his urine drips to the carpeted floor. I grimace beneath my mask.

"Jesus man, get a hold of yourself." Bernard drops him in front of the vault door, thick, gray, and closed. The man's embarrassment takes over; he's now completely silent, on his knees before the vault, only sniffling his draining snot.

"Miss Tiffani! Can you hear me?" Bernard shouts loud enough to frighten most everyone in the bank. Jasmine pauses her gathering briefly behind me, then resumes. "Tiffani, I'm going to assume for this young man's sake that you can hear me! I know you're in the vault and we are running out of time. It was mighty brave, but quite stupid of you, to lock yourself in there."

He pauses, waiting for any response. None comes.

Fuck. I hope she can actually hear us.

"Tiffani, I hate to tell you this but you've put the lives of all your employees at risk by hiding in there. I'm frustrated with you because I *clearly* explained no one would get hurt if you didn't jeopardize our financial goals. Your actions are in direct violation of that and there will be consequences." He's speaking quickly, but with full enunciation. Jasmine is tracking time and I wonder how much of the seven minutes remains.

"I will give you this single opportunity to come out and avoid those consequences. Five seconds." Bernard proposes.

"Four."

"Three."

"Two." There isn't a single sound coming from within.

"One." He pauses an extra second.

"Ok, Tiffani. YOU did this." He bends down to the man who has pissed his pants and whispers. "What's your name?" I stand dumbfounded, wondering what he is doing.

"J-J-Jacob."

"Jacob, I'm going to fire my weapon. It will be loud. The bullet will not hit you, but I want you to scream in pain like it did. You need to sell this or I will actually shoot you to get the reaction I want." The groveling man breathes loudly and deeply. "You got that?"

There is an imperceptible nod among the quivering.

"I need to hear you say it." Bernard speaks softly.

"Y-Y-Yess. Yes. I will."

"Ok good."

Without warning, Bernard fires a round into the ground a foot away. Behind me there are shouts and screams from the other hostages. I jolt as the sound of the discharged weapon echoes to the high ceilings, bouncing around. Jacob yelps initially and briefly, Bernard kicking him gently to remind him of their deal.

"Ahhh arghhhhhh oh my fucking god! My knee! What the fuck did you do to my knee?! Arghhhhhhh" He is laying it on thick, crying perpetually, but it sounds authentic. His life is on the line so it needs to be an Oscar worthy performance. "Tiffani! Please, please come out. He says he's going to do it to my other knee!"

Still nothing.

"Tiffani! Please!" Slobber sprays as he shouts it.

Still nothing. I am growing worried...*was she really in there? She had to be.*

Bernard's voice is much calmer. "Tiffani. That's on you. The next bullet will be too unless you get out here. Is this man's life really less important than the money in that vault?"

"Tiffani! Oh my gawd! Help me!" I feel remorse for him, scared and now learning his boss doesn't give a damn about him.

Bernard fires another shot with zero warning and a similar collective yelp from the hostages rings out. Jacob returns to his award-worthy performance.

"Holllly shit! There's so much blood. Oh my fuck, the painnnnn." He grits through his teeth viciously.

There's a click and Bernard's gaze locks to mine, our weapons trained at the vault door. It swings open, heaving on its hinges and a shameful Tiffani stands there, her mascara running from recent tears. Her already messy hair is even more frazzled.

She only gets three steps outside the vault before Bernard hits her on the back of the head with the butt of his rifle, letting her fall.

Jacob stands slowly and spits toward her. "Fucking bitch, I quit!"

I stifle laughter. Good for Jacob.

Bernard whistles toward Jasmine. "Escort Jacob back to the hostages please."

She nods, takes some cash from the final register and places it in a tactical bag, then grabs Jacob. Before she leaves, she provides an update.

"Four minutes left. Make it snappy."

In a calculated but mad scramble, both of us rush into the vault and begin emptying the cash deposit bags. Just like our intelligence had stated, this SBS branch is housing more than usual as a central pool before a final transport. There's so much cash in sight and transferring it would take too long; we will have to leave a lot of it behind. Potentially the majority of it.

But at least we're in the vault. We can still make it out of this with a worthwhile score to grow our investments with.

"Three minutes." I inform.

Bernard grunts. "Pack faster."

We're slamming stack after stack into our black tactical bags. If there's any tracking on the cash, these will block the signal for the time being, though I doubt a bank of this size could afford that technology. Never hurts to play it safe.

Jazz speaks through the comms. "You've got 30 seconds. Police are incoming, we need to be out those doors in under a minute."

Bernard and I comment simultaneously. "Copy."

By my quick estimate, we've each packed six or seven bags, though it's hard to tell how much money that is because I've seen a wide assortment of bill types. I begin to strategize how I'll carry this out of here. One pack goes along my back and I clasp a second to it. One is on my front, with another clasped similarly. The weight adds up, but the trip to the car is short. My other three bags hang in my hands, dragging my shoulders down, like very heavy, very expensive groceries.

"Leaving." I mention, walking out of the room. This is uncomfortable and my rifle is pressing hard into my ribs. *It's just a short trip.* Jasmine and Jazz see me, and begin backing away from the hostages. She bends down to pick up her single bag packed with the register cash and Jazz calmly keeps his weapon trained on the hostages. I spot Laura still lying motionless against the wall. Bernard's movement catches in the peripherals of my mask while he addresses the unlucky bank employees one last time.

"Well done folks. The police will be here and let you out of the restraints, free to go on with your lives." A variety of scowls look back at him and just like that we exit the large glass doors, back out into the chilly Seattle air. More sunlight has draped the sidewalks and additional cars populate the street. Coming out of a heist is always one of the most nerve-wracking moments because of all the unknowns. Weather, other people, the roads, traffic, random events…you can only plan for so much for it. Luckily, all seems mundane and our cars remain parked outside, running and waiting.

I reach ours first, going to the trunk, able to stash all seven of my bags within. Bernard packs his six in the back seat and quickly joins me in the front.

5:51 AM

My mirrors are clear and 5th Avenue and University has a green light. I slam the transmission to "D" and we're sucked back into the seats with the hum of the motor churning in excitement.

Just another Tuesday morning…

Part V
The Hunter's Surprise

My head hurts like a bitch. What do I remember? Talking with the Mask, telling him to put his gun down…him (or her? Probably him…) refusing. Then nothing.

I come to, expecting to be standing up since that's the last stance I recall. Instead, I'm lying on the hard floor, my back against a wall. Disorientation sets in and I have the urge to vomit, luckily keeping it down by closing my eyes and blinking hard several times.

Around me, there's calm chatter I can barely understand. Phrases come in and out of clarity.

"Everyone ok?" one asks.

"Is Tiffani ok?"

"Who the fuck cares about her?" Followed by a sniffle.

"Jacob…"

Squeezing my core, I roll, trying to get a final survey of my body's positioning. Quickly, I come to realize my hands are bound by something tight, foolishly out in front, as opposed to a much more constricting variation behind my back. Because of this, it's easy to sit up, my nausea being replaced by another sharp pain along the side of my skull.

"Hey, hey!" Some petite feminine voice whisper shouts.

"You don't need to whisper anymore, they're gone." Another chastises.

"Fine, whatever. But she's up!"

"Ughhh. Fuck." I moan and take several additional hard blinks. A deep breath.

"Are you ok? Are you a cop or something?" Her voice is annoying the hell out of me. I open my eyes and finally my vision corrects, providing hard lines instead of blurry ones, only distorted by some tears in the corners of my eyes. I wipe them away with bound hands.

"FBI actually." I remember there are other hostages. "Everyone ok?"

"Yeah…they knocked out our manager, but otherwise we're fine. They said police were on their way."

Something about the past-tense use of the word "said" gains an intense reaction in my belly and my chest. Almost instantly, my pain is gone and my focus heightened.

I have to go after them.

"How long has it been since they left?" I border on shouting.

"What?" The same girl is confused.

"Fuck! How LONG has it been since they –"

"It hasn't been more than a couple minutes. You started coming to right as they walked out the door." I spot a larger security guard, defeated, but understanding the information I need and why.

"Shit!" My gut blazes and there's a tingle across my skin. *I'm still in this.*

Anger-augmented muscles attempt to break the zip tie wrapping my wrists, but it's not budging.

Fuck it, I'll worry about that later.

I'm up, far too quickly, and my world spins, almost dragging me back down to its surface.

"Woah, slow down!" Someone exclaims while I jut a leg out to stabilize myself. Spots dance in my eyes for a couple seconds then dissipate. There's a small chance I have a concussion. My feet are already moving toward the door, running, and I crash into the faux-gold metal exit plunger, into the chilly air and sunlight. I'm thankful for the fall crispness awakening me like a cold shower.

My original hunch about the matching Dodge Charger sedans had been right. They are gone.

"Fuck!" *You can still catch them.* Part of the reason they chose this bank was its proximity to the freeway. *At least I know which direction they were going. There is a chance.*

Ignoring traffic - there's still very little - I bolt to my car and clumsily get in. These zip tie handcuffs have to go. Once more I press against them with all my might, engaging my biceps, shoulders, chest, lats…all of it. *C'mon Laura. What do you workout for if not to break out of handcuffs like the movies?* There's a snap and I briefly, disgustingly, think it's one of my bones, but it's the white plastic, now broken away. I don't take time to celebrate, tossing the trash into the passenger seat, throw my car into drive, and pull a U-turn in the street. An overly-cautious car who is honestly nowhere near me, honks.

Whatever.

I'm off and I don't wait for the light along 5th and University to turn left, heading toward the I-5 on-ramp. Another horn honks and the fiery oranges and muted browns of the sidewalk trees' fall leaves blur beside my vehicle. Annoyingly, there's enough traffic on University to slow me down, and I have to weave between a slow van in the center lane.

Ahead, the light at 6th Avenue is red with one lane, the right one, open. As much as possible, I study the oncoming one-way traffic to make sure I'm not going to fail today because of a simple accident. Cars are approaching, but I can make it, and I shove the gas harder beneath my foot, blowing through the intersection.

In the distance there are sirens. Not for me, but heading to the bank.

Shit response time, boys. Their audible presence makes me ponder what sort of backup I should call for? I quickly choose to hold off until I find the vehicles…*if* I find the vehicles.

Interesting concrete squares, holding foliage and stained with Seattle's perpetual wetness line the right-hand side of the curved I-5 north on-ramp. There's a chance I'm wrong about this, that the matching getaway Chargers are weaving in and out of the downtown grid, but I believe that to be minimal. They'd be fools to not get on the interstate from a bank that's merely two blocks away. And there's only the north ramp along this path…

Quit worrying, Laura. Just fucking drive.

My foot presses harder to the floor, flowing my vehicle down the extended freeway entrance, along and into the early morning Seattle traffic. There's more of it here, with dull black, white, and gray vehicles populating each lane. Maneuvering shouldn't be a problem, but I definitely can't straight line it. I assume they wanted some degree of traffic coverage with their getaway…

Sporadic concrete bridges hang over the interstate, countered by intense blasts of sunlight as I push further north. It's likely that I only have minutes to make up the lost distance they have on me, so I slant to the left lane within moments. Some jackass is lallygagging on this side and I weave aggressively around him, noticing his eyes glued to his cell phone as I do so.

Fucking idiot!

Luckily for the foreseeable distance, I'm clear. Also smart of The Masks, they're *leaving* downtown, not entering it on a morning commute. Traffic is much lighter now that I'm several exits further from the city. 80 miles per hour comes quickly, which is certainly enough to get me pulled over, but I have to chance it. I imagine they're driving careful and inconspicuously, but they had at least a couple minutes on me, maybe more. Enough of the police force uses Dodge Chargers that I know to look for the distinct "racing strip" taillights.

I see none…at least not right now.

There's been no police presence, which is comforting for my speeding ass, but equally annoying that they're missing out on the culprits. But how would they know? Matching vehicles isn't enough to pull someone over…they would have no knowledge about the bank robbery yet.

The thought of backup dances around my skull once more.

Not yet…not yet.

~~~

There's so much going on in my head - thoughts rattling around like popcorn - that the path out of here is a blur. My mask remains over my face and moisture from my breath builds along the cloth interior. Bernard remains silent, for now.

I push the high-powered sedan along the very long entrance ramp to I-5 north, trying to get away from the bank as fast as possible. Jazz and Jasmine are right behind, the distinct headlights of our Dodge Chargers like angry eyes in the dawning sun. Traffic is sparse within the dank tunnel we spit into, and I'm careful to drive aggressive, but measured. Scanning, I don't spot any police. Bernard clears his throat.

"Keep your masks on until I give the all clear. Radio silence until then. If we get police, split up like we discussed." He's just talking to me now. "What the fuck was that, Heath?"

I'm silent. I don't have answers for him.

"Answer the fucking question or the next one there'll be a gun on you." His voice is more gravelly than usual. Darker.

"Look, I have no idea. I've been careful. Her and I have never discussed this side of my life, not once." I think back to her FBI work and the project she can't say much about. "This is a long shot, but this must be the project she's been working on. The one that moved us to Seattle in the first place."

"What the fuck're you talking about. Be clear about it."

I dart to the middle lane, pass two cars clogging up the far left one, and get back in the fast lane. "The reason Laura and I moved here was for a promotion she received and the opportunity to work on a high-security clearance project.
~~~

The only thing I can guess is that it was about bank heists. With us."

"Bullshit." Bernard's terrifying mask nods in exclamation. "The FBI has better things to do. Bigger heist crews to go after. Hell, we've never even killed anyone."

"I don't know what to tell you, Bernard. I don't leave any trail; I'm sure of it. And we certainly don't bank at SBS. I can't think of a single other reason she'd be there that early unless it was related to something she's working on."

"Fuck!" He hits the dashboard hard. "Fuck!"

"Look, I know it's frustrating, but for what it's worth, we got out of there with her none the wiser."

"None the fucking wiser, Heath? We - I - knocked an FBI agent unconscious. Somehow, she's already on our trail. She knew we would be there. I'd say the bitch is *very* wise right now."

"That's my wife you're talking about." Heat builds along my face.

"Exactly. That's *your* wife. I told you this was dangerous years ago. You could have chosen anyone else, but you had to be smitten with the FBI agent."

Both of our anger is spilling over. "Holding that in for a while, have we?"

"You're damn fucking right I have been. I took you in from *nothing* and gave you everything. And I knew this would bite us in the ass one day."

"What do you want me to do, Bernard? Kill my fucking wife?"

There's a disturbing and very dark silence between us.

"Fuck you." I reply to the non-answer. He still doesn't talk and in that heartbreaking moment I make a mental note that Bernard - the pseudo father for a significant chunk of my life - is now an enemy I need to keep tabs on. One who may want to take the person I'm connected with most in this world, my wife, away from me. All because of his paranoia. His greed.

"Slow down." His voice is calmer now with the instruction. I hadn't noticed my foot drifting toward the floor and I lay off it.

Fucking bastard.

Several minutes of silence pass, coupled with the doldrum of driving away from the city.

"Remove the masks. Don't want some random driver noticing and getting spooked." Bernard states into comms. Our entire argument had been off of the group channel, just between us, but I'm apprehensive about what the larger group conversation may be.

As my mask slides off, I didn't realize how stifled I felt behind it. Likely a side effect of my stress levels as opposed to a design flaw.

We're not out of the woods yet, but it has been smooth sailing since we left the building. I perform a thorough scan of every mirror, staring into the rear-view mirror on-and-off for two minutes.

No tails.

No police.

There's another half hour of driving left in these sedans before we cram into a single SUV. While previously driving north, we've now made our way hard right, east, to eventually get closer to the forested coverage of the Pacific Northwest. Rain drops lazily slap onto my windshield, a few here, a few there, and the skies threaten more on the way. I've gotten used to constant rain, but something feels much more ominous about this impending storm. The energy behind it radiates like the man in the seat next to me.

You're projecting, Heath. Calm down.

Silence swallows the rest of our uneventful trip to the cracked and worn parking lot of archaic vehicles where Jazz and I left the SUV. I pull alongside a deserted and heavily graffitied box of a building (my guess is it used to be some sort of convenience store) relieved to find that our final getaway vehicle is still here, untouched. I slow the car,

Bernard stepping out before it's even at a full stop. His anger is palpable…seething. I've never seen him this rattled before.

Jazz and Jasmine pull up behind me, looking mysteriously distant. Like they know something I don't.

Fuck, Heath. What is going on?

The look of concern disappears from their face once we make eye contact and they smile, returning to their normal selves.

"Ay! We fuckin' did it!" Jazz approaches and claps me on the back.

You're imagining things. Calm down.

"There's no one following us whatsoever. It's looking good!" Jasmine comes and gives Bernard and I a hug. I return the gesture, Bernard doesn't, and addresses the group,

"We're not out of the woods yet. Unpack this shit and let's get going." Immediately, the air in the vicinity shifts. Jazz, Jasmine, and I all exchange glances and begin unloading per instructions. We do so in an awkward silence and I'm dreading the trip to the cabin. At least I'll be driving.

Our SUV is a monster - a Suburban - but we'll be riding cozy with the bags of cash piled tightly. Before we leave, Jazz replaces the license plates on the Charger sedans and remotely triggers a device in their computer systems to wipe any stored memory they may have, while also disabling the ignition sequence, making them defunct.

As I suspected, our collective ride in the black, behemoth of a vehicle is awkward and annoyingly silent. Normally at this part of the heist, we're a lively bunch. Fresh off the adrenaline of escaping and high off the excitement of our new found wealth. Elation is the most apt description, but here…here it's apprehension. We all know this heist wasn't our smoothest work, but we still made it out unscathed. Unfollowed.

That Bernard is so angry and on-edge is a rare sight and one the group doesn't take lightly.

Jasmine and Jazz are probably questioning if they should even be proud of what we accomplished today.

I'm an odd combination of guilt-ridden, angry, and frightened. Some part of my consciousness believes what happened today - with my wife - was my fault. But I'm fuming at the thought of Bernard's blame being placed squarely on my shoulders. And I'm frightened of his unspoken solution. That he would even consider it.

To kill. Break his own rule.

My wife.

For the entire drive to the cabin (including a stop to change license plates again and refuel from our gas canisters), those three emotions swirl, like a hurricane of torture, in my gut, chest, and mind. Exhausting me more than the heist ever could have.

~~~

I *fucking* got them.

Two matching Chargers, going north on I-5.

The moment I caught sight of the distinct taillights, my breath hitched. Once I confirmed there were two, right in a row, I was ecstatic.

"I don't believe it." I exclaimed. "I don't believe it." A second time.

My mind was racing, my heart catapulting over and over again within my chest. I felt like a dog chasing a ball and now that I had it, there wasn't much time to decide what to do with it.

Call for backup you idiot! Was plastered like a billboard in my thoughts. Something told me to hold off. I wanted to follow them. I wanted this to be *my* win. Laura Gregory: the FBI agent who brought down The Masks.

At least call Heath. Someone should know what you're doing just in case.

I nearly did. Really. But I didn't even want to share this with him yet. I'm selfish like that, plus he's international, likely asleep right now. I'll tell him later.
~~~

The goal was to just drive. Tail, follow, and stay obscurely in the background. Don't make sudden moves, stay far enough back, and keep track of their likely routes.

That was almost a half hour ago and we've since exited the freeway, leaving me uncomfortably exposed, one of only a handful of cars behind them. Naturally, my heartbeat starts up again and my inner-critic isn't being helpful.

I bet they've spotted me. It chats. *You've been made.*

Luckily, I've gotten good at ignoring that voice, for better or worse. I firmly believe they have no idea who I am or that I'm following them.

After several more minutes, I watch them approaching a stop of some kind, which is confusing because there isn't much around. All I observe is what potentially used to be a gas station - abandoned now - with its well-worn property hosting equally archaic cars, none of which I presume are in use any longer. My decision is made instantaneously and I pull off to the side of the road. Suspicious? Yes. But I'll make it work and they've got bigger concerns on their mind if they just so happen to look back and see a car on the side of the freeway.

My phone goes in my pocket, I take off my FBI jacket, and grab my gun. The goal is to quickly get to the forested area alongside the road before they come to a complete stop. I open the driver door as another car passes distantly in the left-hand lane, its airy rushing sound coming and going without paying me any mind. Rain sprinkles lightly on my hands and forehead, an amount that any Washingtonian can easily ignore, and I book it to the trees.

Their shadows and deep green hues swallow me up and I feel safe again. Comfortably concealed. Still, I must navigate quickly to gain a vantage point of the odd stop they're making. Eventually, I come to the edge of the forest nearest the gas station's building, and take refuge behind a massive, convenient fallen log. The damp wood smells delightful, but I barely register it as I observe the Charger pull forward near the building and stop. I retrieve my phone and switch it to silent mode before opening the camera. Before the car is fully stationary, the passenger side nearest to me sees its door fly open. A statue of a man gets out, silver hair and beard moist from sweat. From the Mask he has since removed.

I'm giddy at my first real glimpse of one of the people underneath the Masks. I begin recording right as the other vehicle pulls up. I notice a SUV parked nearby, black as onyx. *They're switching cars.*

Now I know I need to call this in. It's on camera, I've caught them. Once everyone is out of the cars, I'll be able to put faces to all the names. I've got to call this in.

I've got to call this…

Once everyone is out of the…

My mind takes too many seconds to register what my eyes are gathering.

There's no double or triple take, just pure disbelief.

All four Masks are out of the vehicles, exchanging words and moving quickly to transfer the cash to the Suburban.

But my eyes can't tear away from one of them.

A face that's recognizable, but incomprehensible.

My husband.

Heath.

Is part of The Masks?

Part VI
Worlds Colliding

I have to sit on the damp ground behind the log and catch my breath. Up-and-down, up-and-down my chest heaves, with almost no ability to capture air.

I'm hyperventilating.

My stomach churns and I dry heave to the side. Desperately my body wants something to come up, but nothing does. There's sweat in lots of places and the inside of my mouth feels full of cotton.

Heath…

I try to breathe.

This whole time…

Another attempt. Barely anything.

He robs banks?

Will I pass out?

With The Masks? They've done this a lot.

In the distance, a slamming car door snaps me out of my episode as fast as I entered it. The deeply-seeded FBI "gut" screams at me to focus on the mission still in motion. The soft cackling of rubber tires against wet cement follows and I slowly rise my head above the log.

They're leaving; onto the next leg of their escape plan.

I'm sitting here like an idiot.

Move, Laura!

An urgent glance over the Suburban gives me some final mental notes to remember on the road: it's tinting is significant and I catch a small white scratch along the right side of the back bumper. Then I'm up, sprinting. There's little chance they'll spot me as I run in the opposite direction back to my own vehicle and I must follow them. I'll call in the location of the dual Chargers for evidence, but right now this is about more than just my job.

This has suddenly, violently, and unexpectedly become about my life.

Have the past five plus years been a lie?

Does Heath know I'd been researching his crew? Has he been using me?

Doses of anger, fear, and heartache course throughout me, igniting a stamina I've rarely tapped into. The dead sprint is the fastest I've ever run and I couldn't be further away mentally from the breathlessness and muscle soreness.

In a swift motion, I'm in the car, with it running and my gun tossed onto the passenger seat. My tires spit up gravel like an exclamation to the start of the chase and I swerve back onto the rainy highway without looking, thankful traffic is sparse this deep into the state. Much like I did with the primary getaway vehicles, I search for a black mass, likely driving perfect as possible aside from light speeding.

Anxiety registers quickly as I pass a couple exits they could have easily taken advantage of if they wanted to utilize back roads to their destination, wherever that may be. My gut tells me they're prioritizing speed, trying to get as far away from the center of downtown as possible. It's what I would do…I think?

Your gut isn't worth shit anymore, Laura. You didn't know anything *about Heath.*

I can barely concentrate on driving as the emotions and questions and hurt come back in full force. Raining harder, my windshield is filling with large dots, clear, but obscuring the road. I have to consciously think about how to turn my windshield wipers on - a normally subconscious task - and finally just let out a primal scream. It doesn't form any one word, just a guttural pitch of frustration, filling my cabin that's occupied by only me and myself.

It feels good. I can focus again.

And as soon as I do, their SUV comes into view. A boxy, black thing in the middle lane far ahead, passing an 18-wheeler trudging along. I was right about their direction and about them playing it safe. They could be doing 80 or 100 miles per hour in the left-hand lane, but they're not. Instead, they're smartly weaving through sparse traffic, no one the wiser to the assload of cash on board.

And the criminals that stole it.

And my husband…the criminal.

The thought almost makes me vomit again.

~~~

"So, are we going to address the elephant in the room?" Jasmine's question from the backseat is punchy, looking for a spicy rebuttal. But at least it will get us talking. My excuse is that I've been driving and focusing on getting us out of the metaphorical woods safely, but I know this is about me. As the sole woman in the car, I appreciate her maturity in attempting to guide us down a path toward resolution.

My answer comes after a time. "I don't know what happened. I don't know how she was there." There are no replies and I take it as skepticism; a collective raised eyebrow from the group. "I've been careful. In recent weeks, more than ever." I know part of this is a lie. Forgetting to tell Laura about my "work trip" until it was so late was bad form, sure, but how would she have jumped from that to interfering with our heist? None of the threads are connecting, though I recognize my bias and tunnel vision.

"Mate," Jazz starts. "I believe you. We're brothers, we're all family. But…" the word hits me like a knife in the chest. "There's got to be some explanation. Coincidence is not it. Maybe it would be if we'd been there during normal business hours, but she was there as early as us. Something is off."

"Her office is nearby," I start to reason. "She could have been pulling an all-nighter or getting in early, maybe out for some coffee?"
~~~

"I suppose that's likely, but then why go to the bank?" Jasmine offers.

I shift in my seat, uncomfortably. "The only answer I have for that one is intuition. Maybe she caught a glimpse of us through the windows or the matching vehicles tipped her off?"

Now Jazz alters his position in the back. "I don't know, Heath. These are a lot of jumps in logic we're making."

Bernard has remained silent, stewing. Staring straight out the front of the vehicle. It is a tension-filled response that continues to have us all on edge. Jasmine, once again, braves the storm.

"Bernard, you're awfully silent." There's no question, just an attempt to poke the bear and get it all out in the open. There's a grunt of a reply, an even more awkward rearranging in his seat, and finally his true thoughts.

"I can't trust any of you, least of all Heath, right now." The underlying viciousness that accompanies it shocks the vehicle. I feel it, but Jasmine laughs in the face of it, offended.

"Fuck you, Bernard. None of us are traitors. This isn't some CIA, spy craft bullshit."

"No, maybe not, but it is FBI bullshit. And that's not far off."

"We've done how many heists together, the four of us? Why would we not have betrayed you earlier? Why now?"

"The answer to everything: opportunity."

"What more opportunity is there than what we have right now? We're all worth at least $100 million and you think one of us wants to just throw that away?" Jasmine seethes in anger for the group collectively. "Fuck you, Bernard. Grow up."

He has no rebuttal, but it's obvious she didn't change his mind. I can't add anything…there's nothing more to say, though I fear, driving through a cold drizzle due East, that the fabric of our group is permanently splintered. Frayed, and perhaps broken beyond repair. Tears well in my eyes; this has been my only family and friends for so many years, outside of Laura.

My thoughts morph into something all-consuming about her. A wish I know can never be granted.

I wish she were here now. Meeting everyone…and we could talk this out.

~ ~ ~

The crew I've formally been calling The Masks, have swapped license plates three times since I've been following them, while also filling gas from their own canisters. Realizing my own fuel, I nearly lost them when I drove past to the nearest gas station and frantically filled up, spotting them drive by as I did so.

Now I refer to them as "Heath's Crew" which feels uber weird, but it's all I can think about. We've since crossed into Montana, which their most recent plates match, and I'm wondering how long I'll be following them.

Over the last several hours, my phone has been blowing up, mostly my team asking if I'd seen the news. The Masks had struck in Seattle, not far from our headquarters! My superior sent me a news link that I couldn't tell if it was passive aggressive ("why weren't you able to prevent this?") or showing that he cared by thinking of our project. I've ignored them all. Most importantly I have no texts or calls from Heath. *He's supposed to be international* my logic keeps pestering me, but I know he's right in front of me, after a heist. One that didn't go smoothly. One where his wife was pointing a gun at him.

Oh god…I think back to that moment and nearly vomit. *I could have shot him.* I try to recall my intent in that sequence…would I really have shot that man? The understanding that it was Heath clouds my memory, but I believe I would have. Perhaps not fatally, but still…

I could have shot my husband today.

A confusing sob escapes my chest and tears follow. I don't want to be scared about that, I want to be fucking angry, dammit! Heath has been lying this whole time! I'm hurt.

But I know I love him.

I know I want to figure this out…I think. I don't want to lose him.

People have divorced for far less. You almost shot him, because he's a criminal.

Another sob and leakage of tears come. Quickly, I wipe them away.

"Get your shit together, Laura. Focus." I coach myself. Now's not the time for this, I'm in deep shit, driving through Montana with no backup, pursuing heavily armed bank robbers. Even if my husband is one of them, the danger is real.

After 20 more minutes on the interstate, I watch the black mass take an exit. I've been hanging very far back because their car is easy to spot, which means mine is too. If they're really paying attention, I'd be willing to bet they've clocked me by now, but I can't assume that. I must keep going. As I approach the exit, I watch them angle right, headed toward forested area. We're in a part of the state where stoplights are infrequent and traffic is even rarer. I will need to hang back, letting my intuition guide me.

I take the exit slowly, and eventually the same right turn. They've all but disappeared from view, but luckily that's only because of a bend in the road along the trees, rather than various turn-off choices. An image of an ambush builds in my thoughts; if they were going to do it, this wouldn't be a bad place.

Tepidly, I roll my car forward along the bend. The pavement, partially damp from previous rain, leads like an ominous invitation into the trees. Ahead, daylight quickly becomes shadows, as a tunnel of green swallows the path. There's no SUV in sight, which is mildly panic-inducing, but

I'm grasping how windy the road is. I pray for dirt roads; they're my only chance at spotting tire tracks.

With a little more haste and a little less caution, I accelerate, eager to make sure I don't fall too far behind. It's a dangerous game because should I actually catch up, my vehicle will be the only one on the road. I'll be obvious, and Heath could easily recognize me.

But I can't calculate all the "ifs" and "buts" and "maybes" of this situation. It's impossible to know and I have to go with what I always have: my gut.

My car is an awkward combination of gas and brake, like a teenager learning how to drive. I'm gunning it in between the potential turnoffs, most of which have been dirt, and braking hard to see if there are tire tracks or I can catch a glimpse of taillights in the distance. The forest is inhaling me deeply, the trees pushing me in further, and I'm gradually building doubt that they've evaded me. Places to turn, mostly all long driveways now, are becoming less and less frequent, and none have revealed recent tire tracks.

But then the road transitions from pavement to dirt fully, and my hope is renewed. There are clear, massive tracks along the path. They have to be fresh.

They've been here.

Still, there's no taillights along the winding road, but I'm confident I haven't missed wherever they're going. Which brings up a more significant question: where *are* they going? Some cabin deep in the woods sits ominously at the forefront of my mind as the answer, and I'm worried even more now that I should have reinforcements, or at the very least, someone should know the breadcrumb trail I'm on.

But Heath is there. He wouldn't kill me, would he? Wouldn't let someone else from his crew murder me, would he?

Bumps and divots rattle my car, forcing me to decelerate. This dirt path is not maintained well and I imagine the large SUV, weighed down by cash and people, is having to take things slow too. After ten minutes, it feels like I've been driving forever - because I have - but these last moments are particularly aggravating with all the bumps and steering around deeper holes. Eventually there's some respite. The tire tracks turn left off the road, down a longer driveway that has darker gravel, making it a much smoother ride (though I lose the ability to see their tire grooves).

Peering through the deeply forested ground, there's a large cabin in the distance. The black SUV sits in front, taillights like red beacons of betrayal.

I've got you.

My next decision is an important one and I don't believe there's a right answer:

Do I storm in now, "guns-a-blazing"?

Do I note the spot, turn around and get cell coverage, and phone it in like a good little FBI agent?

Or do I hold off until nightfall, sneak in, and confront my husband covertly?

My mind races back and forth between each option, but my ever-trusty gut narrows in on one.

Nighttime it is.

~~~

The ride to the cabin remained uneventful, but far from boring. Everyone - Jazz, Jasmine, Bernard, and myself - was on edge from the earlier discussion. The only person that spoke was Jazz as he researched the news on his phone.

"Our heist is unsurprisingly today's top story, but the media is reporting there are no leads. Because of the skirmishes with the manager and…erm…FBI agent, we're considered 'armed and dangerous'."

No one replied and my worry deepened a layer further. It felt like the group would not be able to come back from this.

Now that we're in the cabin, matters haven't improved. Bernard is at least talking again, but only for dictating instructions.
~~~

"Each of us get a room. No outside communication yet, and everyone take a few bags of cash with you. We don't want them lying out in the open, just in case. Jazz," He turns to the Australian who has quickly changed into shorts and a hoodie. "Lock this place down tight. We lay low until the heat dies down or we feel the walls closing in." His head nods toward me. "Given everything that transpired, that could very well happen."

"Bernard…" Jasmine says with exasperation. I ignore it while I gather my stuff, including bags of cash, and head toward my room. Walking away, I hear Jazz explaining the security he's put in place.

"There's a rotating drone crew circling the compound with full 360° view, and the home has a security system as well…"

I shut the door behind me, lock it emphatically, raising a dual middle finger salute to Bernard through the wall. I know the majority of people in this cabin are on my side, but I want nothing to do with any of them right now. I toss the bags of cash along the wall and put my small backpack of clothes by the bed, dropping on to its cozy, welcoming embrace.

The urge to text Laura is strong; to play coy and see how her day went. I wonder if she'd mention anything. Of course she wouldn't. It's Laura. She's probably embarrassed about being knocked unconscious. Not to mention, Jazz definitely has a grid over this property, able to see if we're sending any messages in or out. Bernard wanted radio silence and it would only make them more suspicious of me if I broke that. I resolve to deciphering my wife's presence at the bank once we're back together.

In the meantime, fatigue has carefully, slowly woven its silky fingers around me as I lie on the bed. The room (and whole cabin for that matter) is very Montana-esque, if that makes sense, but the ceiling is nothing but dull gray in the darkening space. I triple check my alarm just in case I go completely comatose. It's set for early the next morning.

As I begin to fade into the embrace of sleep, curled on top of the bedsheets, I catch the final murmurs of the group from the large living room. They sound stressed, bordering on argumentative. There will be time for that later, and I only know what I know. For now, I need the disconnect I hope my dreams will provide.

I'm startled awake from a firm pressure across my mouth and nose. Half thinking it's a vivid dream, my eyes are met with the sight of my wife, of Laura, hovering over me with a single finger in front of her mouth. The room is dark and there's a chill from the open window. Slowly, her grip lightens and she backs away, her face a contortion of sadness and intensity. The fog of sleep rips away with a crushing realization:

Laura knows I'm part of the heist.

"How did you…? Why are you…?" They come out as confused whispers, pleading with my wife for answers.

"Shut up and keep your voice down." She walks over to the window and quietly closes it. I feel the heated air from the floor vents trying to keep the large cabin warm.

"Laura, what are you doing here?"

"What am *I* doing here? No, Heath. What are *you* doing here?" Now she's standing over the bed, arms crossed. I feel like a child about to be scolded.

"How did you get in here? Jazz has security…"

She cuts me off. "That doesn't fucking matter right now, Heath. Answer my question." I hang my head.

So this is it. The moment of truth in our marriage that I've been planning toward, here far sooner than I would have liked.

"Okay. Sit." I pat the bed beside me.

"I'll stand thank you."

"Fine…" And I begin to tell my story.

Some parts, like my childhood through college years she's already aware of. Otherwise, I tell her everything from how Bernard recruited me, how I was doing recon for the Austin heist when I first bumped into her, how I'm not really an analyst and that this is my full-time job, that I - sorry, we - are worth upwards of $100 million (she nearly did have to sit for that), that we've had the Seattle heist planned for a couple years, and, regrettably, that I was who she was pointing a gun at.

Her cogs turn, deeply and quickly, in her mind.

"Were *we* real, Heath? Was I just some sort of keep-your-enemies-closer bullshit?"

"Laura, of course n-"

"How long have you known what I've been working on? How long did you know my team and I were studying bank heists? Studying *you*...The Masks."

"Sorry what?" I'm unsure if I heard her correctly.

"At the FBI. The project that moved us here was to study bank heists so we could better prevent them. We called your crew The Masks. They're sort of our white whale."

Talking about work has calmed her down and I can't help but laugh. I do so quietly, still aware of the immediate danger we're both in with her in the room. *Isn't open communication one of the foundational pillars of a happy marriage?*

"The Masks?" I say between chuckles.

"Yes..."

"Not a very clever name, is it?"

A chest-melting smile creeps along her face. "Fuck you."

"Laura, I swear I had no idea what you're working on. There's no sort of double-agent, secret-agenda nonsense between us, I swear. Just a married couple with very conflicting occupations." There's a soft laugh from her between tears. "If anything, it has caused anxiety within this group. They know you work for the FBI and not everyone is supportive of it, Bernard mostly."

I visibly witness the weight lifting from her shoulders hearing me explain this, and understanding it as truth. She knows it is.

"I know I haven't been the best husband." I continue. "I've sat with this secret for a long time and I think it's pushed me further away from you. I didn't want you to find out until I was done…until we had enough that we could run away and never work again." She finally sits next to me on the bed.

"You don't think $100 million is enough to do that?" A solemn expression tells me she has more to say. "I haven't been the best wife either. We've fallen into a rut; I've been way too focused on my work for many years now. I should have known you were going through this. I'm not sure what I would have done…maybe this was the best way to find out…but we've both been keeping too many secrets."

"Well, given mine are highly illegal, there's probably much more fault landing at my doorstep."

"Fair…"

We both sit in the dark room for several minutes, silent, just holding hands as husband and wife. Eventually, Laura asks a question, "So what do we do - "

My phone vibrates on the dresser, cutting her off and lighting the room obnoxiously. I look to her briefly and she must be able to see the concern in my eyes before I lean to check who's calling.

Jazz. *That's weird.* I pick it up.

"Yes?" I initiate.

"Heath, it's Jazz."

"Yes, I know that. It's the middle of the night, what's going on?"

"Please come out of your room, into the main living space." There's a tension in his voice that I don't love. "You *and* Laura."

Fuck. Shit.

"Laura? What do you -"

"Heath, c'mon mate. Don't make us come in there by force." The threat sounds weird coming from his mouth. Almost as if he was told to say it.

Bernard.

"Give us two minutes." I hang up the phone.

"What's going on?" Laura asks, knowing something isn't right.

"They want us to come out to the main living room."

"Why?"

"I'm not sure, Laura." I'm up off the bed by now, rummaging through my personal bag. Without much trouble I find my handgun, check for a bullet in the chamber, and put it in my waistband. "Do you have your gun?" I ask her. She nods.

"Heath, what're we doing?"

"We're going to approach this calmly. There're more people on our side here than not. Jazz and Jasmine aren't going to hurt you."

"What about Bernard?"

"Bernard is a different story after today. Laura, I'm very serious when I say this: do not tell them what you're working on. Explain to them today was a coincidence in passing by. Wrong place, wrong time. You'll need to convince them - him - that you could leave the FBI."

"*Leave* the FBI? Are you fucking joking?"

"I'm not. And you have to know it's true. How do we return to our normal lives after today? How do *you* return to your job?"

There's a moment of shock, coming to terms with a realization she'd already been subconsciously toying with.

"I'm sorry I put you in this position. It was selfish of me. There's plenty more to figure out, but for right now, we need to be convincing to make it out of here alive."

As if I'm entering enemy territory, I ease the door open. No one is waiting for us - I was half expecting an ambush the moment the door unlocked - but there's the glow of late-night lamp light coming from the main part of the majestic cabin.

"Let me go first." I whisper back to my wife.

As I pass the threshold of the room into the main living space, I wonder if I should raise my hands? Does that imply guilt? I decide against it and am greeted by Jazz sitting on the oversized brown leather sofa, with Jasmine standing nervously nearby.

"Where's Bernard?" I inquiry while I step further into the room. Jasmine's eyes look past me painfully, and she turns away.

"Heath…" There's a shake in my wife's voice.

The image I'm met with sends my synapses firing, unsure of how to respond, but only for a half moment. After that brief peak of overload, they shout *Get your gun out!* And I obey.

Bernard stands next to my wife, gun pointed at her head, staring at me.

My weapon is trained on him.

Laura knows that if she pulls her gun, Bernard will put her down.

"Bernard, put down the fucking gun. Now." It comes out calmly, like I intended, but full of bite along the edges. The man's massive forearms seemingly pulse at my instruction, the veins twitching with a "No".

He's not sure what happens next. He planned this intervention, without understanding the consequences. I shoot a glance over my shoulder to my friends - or those whom I believed to be friends - and their faces are colored with shame.

"Bernard, what are you going to do?" I press. "Are you going to shoot Laura?"

There's no answer, just wild eyes and his shifting grip on the gun. Laura's fear has subsided, now visible anger, as she glances between the two of us, hands in the air.

"If you shoot her, I will kill you. You've taken this too far." My explanation is measured. He already knows this.

"She's an FBI agent. She will give us all up in a second, including you, Heath."

Laura tries to clarify. "I won't. I swear. I was passing by on accident and saw what was happening…I-"

"I cannot believe you, and it doesn't really matter. Your job, your oath, would be to report us." Bernard reasons, convinced he is on the right path. "This was not some small-potatoes gas-station robbery. We're a full-fledged heist crew."

Laura knows he's right and doesn't try arguing. The tension in the room balances on the edge of a knife. Heartbeats are practically audible as the anticipation for gunshots mounts. Bernard looks to me.

"I told you…I told you this was risky." There's a deep emotion in his tone. "Anyone else, Heath! Anyone else and we wouldn't have to be doing this right now!"

"I kn-" I attempt.

"You don't fucking know! Otherwise, you would have fucking listened to me!" Bernard is screaming.

"Bernard, c'mon. Just put the gun down and let's all talk this through." Jasmine reasons with both frustration and fear.

"You all know I'm right! Heath has *ruined* us. Over a decade of building our wealth, *gone!*"

"Bernard, nothing is gone." Jasmine counters. "All our money is still there. This only means we all need to come to an agreement and lay low for longer before the next heist."

Bernard scolds her like a father. "Jasmine, sit the fuck down." There's a "tsk" from Jazz.

"Excuse me?"

There's a tense, awkward silence now, but Jasmine backs down without taking a seat.

"What're you going to do Bernard? Do you want to fully dismantle this family from something you can never come back from? Or sit down and talk this out…find a solution?"

Laura's stance shifts from tense and pent-up, toward a place of relaxed understanding. "Please," she starts. "There is a solution where we all come out of this alive."

Bernard thinks for a long moment. Perspiration drips down my side from holding the gun for several minutes. Out in the woods, some animal makes a faint noise.

"But there's only one solution where I don't have to be looking over my shoulder for the rest of my life."

Laura's face has finally transitioned to fear and from her perspective I sense she saw something - some shift - in Bernard's eyes.

"Jesus…" Jasmine mutters, worried, under her breath behind me.

Enough of this. I have enough money to last a lifetime. It's clear Bernard is alone in this room.

The next few seconds are equally a blur and distinctly clear. My finger presses the trigger and there's an odd sensation as my aim drifts. The eruption from the gun overtakes everything in the room, barely escaped from my own barrel before Bernard's gun follows suit. In the aftermath of the firearms discharging, there's a brief second of confusion before the chaos.

Bernard lies on the floor, blood pouring from his neck with a soft gurgle. Laura has similarly fallen, writhing in pain, shouting. I rush to check on her while Jasmine does the same with Bernard.

"Oh my God! What did you do?" She shouts. A stolen glance toward Bernard before I reach Laura shows his eyes plastered with wide-eyed shock. He's dying. Laura continues to moan through gritted teeth and upon approach there's a bullet hole leaking a considerable amount of blood in the center of her upper right arm.

"Fuck, oh fuck. That hurts like a bittttt…" She grips her upper arm hard, but it's not doing much.

"Here, hold on." I remove my shirt and tie it around the wound. "Stay here." Quickly, I dart into my room, snag a belt, and run back out to my wife. The collective amount of blood loss in the air gives the room a haunting, metallic scent. I wrap the belt around her upper arm above the hole. It may only help a little, but it's better than nothing.

Jasmine has similarly removed her shirt, pressing it against Bernard's neck. "Jazz get the fuck over here and help me!" Jazz, white as a ghost, timidly approaches the grisly scene.

"What can I do?" He asks, unsure if he wants the answer.

"Hold this right here, against his neck. Tightly." Her hands are covered in Bernard's crimson and Jazz takes over, pressing on the soaking shirt. I've been slowly helping Laura sit up, recognizing that we have to leave. Now. My gaze meets Jasmine's and there's an unspoken understanding between us.

"Both of them need to go to a hospital." I state the obvious. "We should go in different directions. Laura will likely last longer."

Jasmine is on her phone, searching hospitals on the map. "We'll go north from the interstate, that's the closest one. You've got a bit of a drive, but you can go back west about an hour."

"Jasmine…I…" It's hard. I don't even know what to say for just blowing up our family. Permanently. I had no choice.

"I know." She seems like she wants to say more. "I know. Look, just take what money is in your room and go. You can't ever come back, but at least the two of you can run away. Start a life somewhere new."

"Thank you." I help Laura stand. She grunts, but it's clear the pain is evening out. "What about Bernard?"

"I don't know, Heath. He'll probably die. But if he doesn't, maybe this whole interaction will provide him some perspective. I'll do my best to convince him to leave you two alone, but that's why you have to run."

"I know." It's becoming increasingly clear these are the last words I'll have with them. With my family. "Thanks Jasmine. Thanks Jazz. Stay safe please."

Jasmine smiles while Jazz is preoccupied with keeping Bernard's blood inside his body. Laura leans against the blood-spattered wall and I quickly gather all the belongings - and cash - from my room.

"Can you walk?" I ask my wife. Laura nods with a distant stare. She's not doing well, but we'll make it. She grips her arm while I carry the cash and my belongings toward the front door. I take one final look back at the family I'll never see again. Perhaps I did destroy this group? At the end of it all, maybe it was all my doing.

Laura takes my shoulder with a squeeze. "C'mon, Heath." There are layers of empathy there…of coming to terms with what this means for both of us.

And with that, we cross the threshold of the doorway, leaving my life as a heist criminal behind forever.

~~~

I've honestly still not come to terms with it all. Leaving my career abruptly. All the money. Running away with Heath. Strangely, about the only thing I've actually moved on from is that I was shot in the arm. It hurt like a bitch, and the long, nighttime drive to the hospital was rough, but it all worked out with minimal permanent damage and it is healing well.

This transition hasn't been easy. I abruptly quit the FBI, citing "workplace trauma" from the heist, feeding them some line about how it "put things into perspective" for me. I'm not sure they bought it and they're probably going to track my whereabouts…until we lose them.

My family was a little more accepting of that story, so Heath and I had a family Zoom meeting with my parents and Jason, to let them know we'd be taking some time to travel. They were happy for us, though I wonder if Jason could tell something was off? Someday we'll tell them the truth because there'll be questions about how we can afford everything, but for now they're just glad I'm okay.

Heath has been in a rough space though. Among all the chaos of quickly packing up our lives, he's been quiet. Sullen. And a bit scared. I imagine the fear comes from a multitude of angles. Did he kill Bernard, his father figure? If not, is Bernard going to be crashing through our door at any moment? And strangely the most distant question: the heist didn't go well…could they be caught? Could the police be coming for him too? But that's not what scares *me* most. My
~~~

newfound fear is that I've ruined my husband's life, which is awfully unfair to me given that he was a high-profile criminal (I'll unpack that later), but I can't help but feel responsible for all of this. I can't help but believe I brought this upon our marriage. I can't help but sense that Heath now hates me, deeply, perhaps subconsciously. I don't dare broach all of these topics with him until we're settled with our new lives, but they're conversations we must have and, disgustingly, I hope our new, lavishly-financed "normal" will take the sting out of everything. It's over $100 million for fuck's sake!

I can't wrap my head around how we have that much money.

Today, we're laying low at a fancy hotel in Denver, and we have a talk with the "Advisor". Heath has since explained many facets of the bank heist crew - one being that they were definitely *not* called "The Masks" - and the financial Advisor is the one who has arguably made them all their money. Heath is nervous because he's not sure how it will go after everything that happened in Montana. He's unsure of where the Advisor's loyalties lie, or if he really has any.

The phone rings once and the mysterious voice picks up, "Hi, Heath. How's it going?"

"Hi, sir. It's going okay. Have you heard from the others yet?"

"I have not. But I figure I will soon given that the heist seemed to be successful." The voice pauses, sensing more in the silence. "What's up?"

"Well, there's a lot to tell. I should also mention I have my wife on the line with us. I hope that's ok?"

"I presume she's aware there's no way to track me even if she wanted to? And...I'm guessing something fairly dramatic has occurred if she's in the fold." It's a statement, not a question. The guy is perceptive.

"Yes. The heist didn't go entirely smooth, but we made it out with plenty of cash. My wife, Laura, has been investigating our crew completely unaware that I was part of it, and through a wild stroke of bad luck, she was at the bank that morning. Long story short, Bernard knocked her out, blamed and accused me of betraying everyone, Laura showed up at our safehouse because she followed us and…I shot Bernard. Bernard shot her. We ran away and we're both retiring." The last bit comes out rushed, as if he doesn't want to relive it.

"I see…"

"Look, I know you're loyal to Bernard. I know you don't need to help me…*us.*" Heath explains. "But I'd really appreciate it if you could help us get set up elsewhere. Then you never have to hear from me again."

"Heath, while I don't appreciate messy situations and the risk they introduce, I'm loyal to my *clients.* You are my *client.* I'll continue to support you, just as I will continue to support Bernard, Jasmine, and Jazz with their funds." There's a small laugh. "Plus, this isn't even the messiest situation I've seen. Some of my other clients…" He lets the statement drift. I witness a massive weight lift from my husband's shoulders.

"Thank you, sir. Thank you."

"And what about you Mrs. Gregory? Are you done with the FBI?" I'm shocked he's addressing me, but in a way, I'm the elephant in the room.

"I…I am, sir. Heath and I have a lot to work through, but this is more important than my career. I'll miss it, but…" I'm not sure what else there is to say, so I let my sentence trail off.

"Okay good. My unsolicited advice was going to be that there's no going back to your old lives after this, but it seems you've both come to terms with that. And the good news is you've got a *lot* of money and I'm looking forward to making it work hard for you so you can make *a lot more.*"

The Advisor and Heath continued to talk through logistics, including how to funnel the Seattle heist cash cautiously, and it suddenly hit me: *Laura, you're a multi-multi-millionaire.*

~~~
~~~

Half a year has passed and honestly? Laura and I are closer than ever. Despite her being in the FBI and my history of robbing banks, this feels like the biggest adventure of our lifetimes, and our marriage is all the better for it. Gone are the secrets, which in turn has eliminated the boredom. We're getting to enjoy the world, and *explore* its cultures, together. Sure, we look over our shoulder from time to time, her for the FBI, myself for a Bernard whom I'm not sure is dead or alive, but time is a remedy. The more days, weeks, and months that pass, the more excited we both become to discover each other again, discover *us* further, and enjoy the fruits of our labor.

The Advisor makes us so much money every month that, even with both of us not working, we're still growing our net worth. It's a nice problem to have and I know eventually we'll get bored. Eventually we'll want more to life, maybe jobs again, or maybe a hobby (painting? writing?) to pass the time but for now, the prolonged sabbatical is what we both had no idea we needed.

We're in Croatia now, near the cusp of summer, and loving the hell out of it. I think we'll stay here to enjoy the beaches, the weather, the food, and the varied assortment of tourists from all over the world. Our weeks consist of leisure, taking boat rides along the miraculous coast, hiking in search of pristine ocean views, working out, reading, having slow cups of morning coffee, mid-morning sex, late lunches, afternoon naps, and late dinners. Weekends are an assortment of shopping, finding the best cocktail lounges and speak-easies, dancing with the locals, dancing with the tourists, more sex, and sleeping in.

It's all a dream, and one that I get to share with my wife. And the best part?

I see no reason at all why it has to end.

This is why I did what I did. To create this life for her. For us.

The both of us, forever.

Epilogue
A Foe's Fulcrum

It was nearing the rainy season in Positano, Italy. Despite that, the weather at the start of October was uncharacteristically warm and stunning. Great for the Amalfi Coast's tourism industry, somewhat bad for him. He'd anticipated it being less crowded.

The drink of choice around here was either limoncello or an Aperol Spritz, neither of which sounded appealing. Instead, he ordered a bottle of red wine, leaving the specifics up to the friendly waitress. Along with his pizza - *when in Rome, right?* - the wine was effortlessly exquisite. That was the thing about Italy; the food was flat-out miraculous. Pizzas and pastas you'd remember eating 20 years from now, wines that linger on the tongue, desserts that bury into your core memories…he'd been secretly appreciative that roads had led here.

Roads that had been five years in the making.

The thought sent a swift, corkscrew of pain through Bernard's neck. Short, but jagged. There, but not. The place where Heath had shot him without thinking twice. It was the physical manifestation of the crew's dismantling…an end to the thing he'd been most proud of in his life.

Somehow, he'd survived that night, thanks in large part to Jasmine. He lost a lot of blood, and had been in the hospital for a week. Police came sniffing around since it was a gunshot wound, but he'd been able to play it off with minimal suspicion. No one had made the connection to the Seattle bank heist - which he felt was very lucky - so once he was healed and ready for discharge, Bernard was a free man.

Jasmine and Jazz had vacated the cabin, cleaning it furiously and wiping every trace they could find of their presence. They'd taken the last amount of cash with them and the group agreed to meet in South Dakota to return Bernard his share. The group, minus Heath.

Bernard thought back to his scalding anger those first days out of the hospital. Penetrating every thought, visible in his eyes. Heath had *ruined everything*, and was running away. Hiding. And even took money with him! There was disappointment in his protégé too, but the madness of it all was primary. It traveled with him to South Dakota where Jasmine seemed somber and disconnected. Jazz was probably annoyed more than anything. They'd given Bernard his money and explained how they laid low after bolting from the cabin.

Then Bernard had asked, pried, if the crew would stay together. Three, instead of four now. They'd done it before. Why not again?

"Bernard, I don't think so." Jasmine winced as she said it. Jazz was avoiding eye contact, letting her do the talking for both of them.

That anger remained on Bernard's breath. "Why not?"

"Because I saw a side of you…" She choked up a bit before continuing. "I saw a side of you that I never want to see again. You're dangerous."

You're dangerous.

The words and that meeting echoed with him now. A memory come in from the cold, planting itself in his thoughts. That had been the end of their bank heists. Bernard couldn't do these alone and he'd debated forming a new crew for a long time, eventually coming to the conclusion that it would just be a quick way to end up dead or in jail.

There were no other people he trusted. And Heath had ruined that. Heath and his FBI wife.

Of course he was mad.

Of course he wanted *revenge.*

Sure, the money was still there. The Advisor kept it growing. But his *family* - the one that he had built - was ripped away from him. Without remorse or an apology.

As it had at various points in the last five years, the anger translated into a massive swig of deep purple wine, bursting with luscious flavor. More splashed from the bottle into his glass like an ocean wave. Another sip, smaller this time, was taken before ripping a chunk of pizza from the massive pie.

Bernard refocused on what he'd come here to do.

To kill Heath and Laura.

To tie up the final loose ends.

The delicious, busy restaurant afforded an excellent, elevated view toward the Tyrrhenian Sea and the postcard-worthy beaches leading to it. Along their shores, couples held hands, ate gelato or lemon slush, and took their pictures in front of the picturesque and delightfully pastel-colored homes built into the coast's cliffs. The sun hung high in the nearly cloudless sky; a perfect day for swimming near the end of this summer season.

And that's exactly what Heath and Laura were doing here, revisiting the place they'd taken their honeymoon. He'd been searching for them a long time, eventually finding them in Croatia, now on vacation in Italy.

What a life, you bastard.

Both of them looked happy. Healthy.

Heath smiled at his wife and she let out a laugh that Bernard could just make out from his seat. The kind of distant sound that blends into the background unless you're looking right at the source.

And then something unexpected.

Between them, a baby stood, wobbly on their beach towel. He wore a blue swim diaper and had a mocha mix of their skin tones. For a moment, he thought he had balance and dared to take a step forward, missing it completely, and falling into Laura's arms. Heath let out a hearty laugh this time, beaming from ear to ear. Bernard couldn't tell what he said to the baby, but it looked like, "Nice try, buddy." He kissed Laura and both of them relaxed on their beach setup, facing the shine and waves of the ocean.

Bernard didn't think this changed anything.

It changes everything, you idiot.

Another couple heavy gulps of wine went down his gullet. An aggressive bite of pizza.

His life was good. He was absurdly rich, eating and staying wherever he wanted to in the world. Currently in the slice of heaven that is Positano, Italy. He'd lived his past life, the bank heists.

Maybe it is time to let this go…

Maybe…

Acknowledgements

The Mask of a Marriage originally started as a "freebie" idea related to some marketing. Yes, it ultimately serves that purpose, but I am so damn glad I took the plunge.

After writing something as beefy and complex as *Infinitude*, this was a nice palette cleanser and flowed from my mind to the page easily. I knew it was an idea I didn't have enough for a full book, but that was also the best part. Writing short(ish) stories is a blast and this has turned me on to a new realm of ways I could tell stories if I don't have an idea that fills 300+ pages.

Since this is a "short" story, I'll similarly keep my acknowledgements short with less pomp and circumstance than I usually do.

Molly – per usual, your interest in this story and my hobby as a whole are beyond supportive. It can be a time sink, but you're always interested to hear more and ask how you can help in addition to beta reading duties. I love you!

Lexi – you're an incredible editor and I love working with you every time we get the opportunity. I know life is busy, especially when this one was ready for review, so I appreciate the willingness to fit it in. Beyond the editing, your words of encouragement always mean a ton as well – thank you!!

And in case you were wondering, yes…even short stories need beta readers. Thomas, Bekkah, and Gary – thank you so much for taking the time to give this a shot. Your thoughts caught many broader things I hadn't considered, as well as the smaller stuff, like meaningful logistics. I appreciate your support and feedback more than you know.

As always – **YOU!** I'm passionate about writing and passionate about reading, and I hope that if you're a long time, avid reader, that this story excited you. And if you're getting back into reading, welcome! I hope this makes you want to read more. The fact that you chose to read something of mine is truly humbling.

About the Author – J.T. Rath

J.T. Rath has had a passion for writing since he was in the 5th grade. In high school, he was given an opportunity to write a 5-page short story that ultimately turned into 20 pages and the prologue (of sorts) to his first novel, *Agents & Angels.* That action-packed story, set in the world of spies, had an even more exciting follow-up, *Agents & Angels II: The Wolfpaw Initiative* that concluded the tale. Both can be purchased on Amazon.

The Mask of a Marriage is J.T. Rath's first short story and fourth writing project. His sprawling, intense, sci-fi epic, *Infinitude* releases in 2024.

J.T. Rath lives and works in Denver, Colorado with his wife, Molly, and their Bernese Mountain Dog, Barley. In his free time, J.T. Rath reviews movies and videogames that can be found on his blog: www.raths-reviews.com

He loves hearing from fans and fellow writers and encourages anyone interested to reach out to him at his email j.t.rath.author@gmail.com, find him on Facebook and Instagram, or via his website, www.jtrath.com.